ABOUT THE AUTHOR

Barbara Cartland, the world's most famous romantic novelist, who is also an historian, playwright, lecturer, political speaker and television personality, has now written over 550 books and sold over 600 million copies all over the world.

She has also had many historical works published and has written four autobiographies as well as the biographies of her mother and that of her brother, Ronald Cartland, who was the first Member of Parliament to be killed in the last war. This book has a preface by Sir Winston Churchill and has just been published with an introduction by the late Sir Arthur Bryant.

"Love at the Helm" a novel written with the help and inspiration of the late Earl Mountbatten of Burma, Great Uncle of His Royal Highness The Prince of Wales, is being sold for the Mountbatten Memorial Trust.

She has broken the world record for the last sixteen years by writing an average of twenty-three books a year. In the Guinness Book of Records she is listed as the world's top-selling author.

Miss Cartland in 1978 sang an Album of Love Songs with the Royal Philharmonic Orchestra.

In private life Barbara Cartland, who is a Dame of Grace of the Order of St. John of Jerusalem, Chairman of the St. John Council in Hertfordshire and Deputy President of the St. John Ambulance Brigade, has fought for better conditions and salaries for Midwives and Nurses.

She championed the cause for the Elderly in 1956 invoking a Government Enquiry into the "Housing Conditions of Old People".

In 1962 she had the Law of England changed so that Local Authorities had to provide camps for their own Gypsies. This has meant that since then thousands and thousands of Gypsy children have been able to go to School which they had never been able to do in the past, as their caravans were moved every twenty-four hours by the Police.

There are now fourteen camps in Hertfordshire and Barbara Cartland has her own Romany Gypsy Camp called Barbaraville by the Gypsies.

Her designs "Decorating with Love" are being sold all over the U.S.A. and the National Home Fashions League made her in 1981 "Woman of Achievement".

Barbara Cartland's book "Getting Older, Growing Younger" has been published in Great Britain and the U.S.A. and her fifth Cookery Book, "The Romance of Food" is now being used by the House of Commons.

In 1984 she received at Kennedy Airport, America's Bishop Wright Air Industry Award for her contribution to the development of aviation. In 1931 she and two R.A.F. Officers thought of, and carried the first aeroplane-towed glider air-mail.

During the War she was Chief Lady Welfare Officer in Bedfordshire looking after 20,000 Service men and women. She thought of having a pool of Wedding Dresses at the War Office so a Service Bride could hire a gown for the day.

She bought 1,000 secondhand gowns without coupons for the A.T.S., the W.A.A.F.s and the W.R.E.N.S. In 1945 Barbara Cartland received the Certificate of Merit from Eastern Command.

In 1964 Barbara Cartland founded the National Association for Health of which she is the President, as a front for all the Health Stores and for any product made as alternative medicine.

This has now a £650,000,000 turnover a year, with one-third going in export.

In January 1988 she received "La Medaille de Vermeil de la Ville de Paris", (the Gold Medal of Paris). This is the highest award to be given by the City of Paris for ACHIEVEMENT – 25 million books sold in France.

In March 1988 Barbara Cartland was asked by the Indian Government to open their Health Resort outside Delhi. This is almost the largest Health Resort in the world.

Barbara Cartland was made a Dame of the Order of the British Empire in the 1991 New Year's Honours List, by Her Majesty The Queen for her contribution to literature and also for her years of work for the community.

Hiding

Carita Wensley's mother dies and her Stepfather informs her that she is to marry Lord Stilbury who is a very old man.

Because he is a social snob her Stepfather is determined she will do so and knowing he is her Guardian by law Carita runs away to hide from him.

She takes with her a spirited horse which she hopes will carry her to Norfolk where her eccentric Uncle lives.

She is wondering where she can stay the night when suddenly over a hedge a man on a magnificent stallion appears only to land in a gravel pit and, hitting his head on a stone, lies unconscious.

Knowing she must do something to help him Carita hails a farm-cart which is being drawn down a nearby lane by two lads.

They lift the unconscious stranger into the cart and take him to the farm-house where the farmer's wife, a pleasant, kindly woman assumes that he and Carita are man and wife.

Carita does not contradict her supposition because having nowhere to stay and being afraid her Stepfather will catch up with her, she knows she would be expected to stay near her 'husband'.

Later when the stranger recovers consciousness she tells him of the woman's mistake and begs him not to tell her the truth.

She learns that he too is hiding, having escaped from a woman by constructing a rope-ladder out of his bed-clothes because she is trying to trick him into marriage for his title and his money.

He therefore does not tell Carita who he really is and accepts the situation.

They journey on together to where he thinks he might find her accommodation in the village which he owns.

How there is once again danger from the woman who is still pursuing him, and also for Carita from her Stepfather.

How they both escape by finding a joint solution to their problems is told in this exciting 459th book by Barbara Cartland.

BARBARA CARTLAND

Hiding

Mandarin

A Mandarin Paperback

HIDING

First published in Great Britain 1992
by Mandarin Paperbacks
Michelin House, 81 Fulham Road, London SW3 6RB

Mandarin is an imprint of the Octopus Publishing Group,
a division of Reed International Books Limited

Copyright © Cartland Promotions 1992

A CIP catalogue record for this title
is available from the British Library
ISBN 0 7493 0798 6

Typeset by Falcon Typographic Art Ltd,
Edinburgh & London
Printed and bound in Great Britain
by Cox & Wyman Ltd, Reading, Berks

AUTHOR'S NOTE

The cry of 'Stand and deliver' struck terror into the hearts of travellers in 17th to 19th century England.

This was the cry of the Highwaymen until the horse patrols and police patrols made it harder for them to rob rich people in their carriages.

Dick Turpin is one of the best-known of English Highwaymen who to-day is looked on as a romantic figure.

However in May 1793 he murdered a Keeper of Epping Forest who tried to capture him and for this a reward of £200 was put on his head.

He was a butcher by trade, aged about thirty, and described as being 'very much marked with the small-pox'.

He was eventually executed at Tyburn where public hangings were held well into the 19th century.

Legends have grown up around these men and one of them was Dick Turpin's ride to York on a horse called Black Bess – a ride he never took on a horse he never owned.

CHAPTER ONE
1823

The Earl of Kelvindale felt a soft body move against his.

He had been asleep, which was not surprising.

His love-making with Lady Imogen Basset had been fiery, passionate and extremely exhausting.

He had arrived at her house after a long and tiring drive from London.

He hoped he could have an early night – alone.

However, he had been dismayed to discover she had a large and somewhat rowdy house-party.

It included her two brothers whom the Earl knew to be thoroughly disreputable.

They were continually gambling for stakes higher than they could afford, which meant they were always in debt.

They also drank too much, and had been involved in one social scandal after another.

By the time dinner was over he decided he had made a mistake.

He should not have accepted Lady Imogen's invitation.

Because he was so important and a member of one of the oldest families in the country as well as being excessively rich, he was deluged with invitations.

He was welcome in every house in the land and was *persona grata* at Court.

He had found himself where Imogen was concerned, the hunted rather than the hunter.

Undoubtedly the most beautiful woman in the *Beau Monde*, she was pursued relentlessly by all the Bucks and Beaux who clustered round George IV.

That her amorous engagements rivalled those of the King only added to her appeal.

She could therefore pick and choose a lover from a large number of applicants, and made the most of it.

She had however recently set her sights on the Earl and began determinedly to stalk him.

He had at times felt like a hunted stag or a running fox.

At the same time Lady Imogen intrigued him.

She was so outrageous, so witty, and so ready to mock at herself that he found her amusing.

He had always been extremely discreet in his love-affairs.

He disliked being the butt of the Cartoonists as the King had been ever since he was Prince of Wales.

He also tried to avoid as far as possible the gossip and chatter of social tongues.

This however was, where he was concerned, impossible.

He was far too handsome and too much of a matrimonial catch.

Every woman of any importance desired him either for herself or as a son-in-law.

He had driven to Imogen's Country house in his latest travelling-chariot drawn by four superb horses.

His horses were always envied by every owner and breeder in the land.

One of the lures which Imogen had used to entice him to stay with her had been the promise of a Steeple-Chase.

It was something which the Earl always enjoyed and was invariably the winner.

He had therefore sent ahead of him two of his best and fastest horses so that they would be fresh for the contest.

He had never before stayed at *The Towers* where Imogen had lived with her husband when he was alive.

She had married when she was seventeen.

Already she had displayed some of her amazing beauty, which was to make her the toast of every Club in St. James's.

Her choice was unfortunate for Richard Basset, although a Gentleman, was only a third son.

He therefore had very little money.

He had, however, fallen in love with Imogen on sight and because he was so handsome in his uniform she had melted into his arms.

She swore that if she was forbidden to marry him they would elope.

Her father, the Duke of Bredon had reluctantly allowed the marriage.

It had ended, perhaps fortunately, after five years when Richard Basset was killed in a duel defending his honour.

He had obstinately refused to believe that his wife had been unfaithful to him.

He 'called out' the man who was boasting of his affair with her.

However, and it was an unusual outcome of such duels, he was mortally wounded in the heart.

The victor had to flee the country for at least three years.

Imogen was free, and at the height of her beauty.

Her father gave her enough money to have a house in London.

She took what she required for her gowns and her jewels from her lovers.

By the time she was twenty-seven she had begun to think it was time she secured her future.

She was intelligent enough to realise that beauty, however spectacular, would not last for ever.

If she was not careful she would be replaced by one of the new Beauties.

They all tried to climb up onto the pedestal on which she now reigned supreme.

When she met the Earl of Kelvindale for the first time she knew he was exactly what she required.

Of course she had heard of him.

It would have been impossible to be a part of the *Beau Monde* and not learn of his racing successes and his amorous adventures.

All of these had been with beautiful but discreet women.

They made it difficult for those who spied on them to be able to prove that what they suspected was the truth.

But Imogen had no intention of 'hiding her light under a bushel'.

As soon as the Earl had succumbed to her advances she proclaimed it loudly to all and sundry.

He was not aware of this at first and, when he was, it made him extremely angry.

He accused Lady Imogen of behaving vulgarly, but she had merely laughed at him.

"Why should you be ashamed of our association?" she asked. "I am proud of it, Darol, and you know as well as I do there is no couple in the world more handsome than we are when we are together!"

Because she was so frank about it the Earl found himself laughing.

At the same time he told himself that things had gone a bit too far, and the sooner he withdrew the better.

He had however found it difficult to extract himself.

He had promised quite casually that one day he would visit *The Towers* and take part in a Steeple-Chase.

Imogen assured him the course was one of the most demanding in the whole country.

"The last time I had one," she related, "half the riders were unable to complete it, but I know that you, dearest, when you win the silver cup I am giving to the winner, will show them what inferior equestrians they are."

The Earl thought this was a somewhat sweeping statement.

He knew that two of his friends who would be competing were outstanding riders.

He had therefore left London early in the morning.

He had sent three changes of horses ahead two days previously.

With really expert driving he could reach *The Towers* in time for dinner.

He had achieved it with a quarter-of-an-hour to spare.

At the same time, although he did not like to admit it, he was quite tired.

Both physically and mentally.

The concentration of driving not only on the main roads but also along twisting narrow lanes had won him the admiration of his grooms.

"No 'un but ye, M'Lord, could 'ave done it!" his head Groom exclaimed as they arrived at *The Towers*.

But as he lay in a warm bath before dinner he hoped the evening would not be a long one.

His hopes were not to be realised.

When he eventually got into bed he sank down wearily against the soft pillows.

He told himself he must sleep at once if he was to be on form for the Steeple Chase.

He thought as he closed his eyes that he had learnt very little about it during the evening.

He was not even aware of what time it was to start.

Now that he thought about it, it seemed as if everybody present had deliberately refrained from talking about what was taking place the following day.

He wondered if Imogen was up to one of her tricks.

Perhaps she had contrived a different sort of Steeple-Chase from those that had taken place before.

It would be like her to insist that the riders were blindfolded or only allowed to use one arm.

"If that is what she is thinking of doing," the Earl told himself, "I am damned if I will take part!"

It was then he heard the door open and to his astonishment Imogen came in.

She had pursued him relentlessly.

She had made certain they stayed together in different houses so that they could spend the nights in each other's company.

But she had never until this moment come to his room.

It was an unwritten law that it was the men who went to the women's room when they were conducting an *affaire de coeur*.

Now she appeared carrying a candle in her hand.

She looked, he realised, extremely alluring in a diaphanous nightgown which revealed rather than concealed the perfection of her body.

Her long dark hair fell over her shoulders nearly to her waist.

Her eyes, which had a touch of green in them, glinted like the eyes of a tigress.

"Imogen!" the Earl exclaimed. "Why are you here?"

She laughed a silver laugh which had been described by all of her admirers as being like a peal of bells.

"I should have thought that was obvious, Darol!" she replied.

She put the candle down on the bedside table and stood beside the bed looking at him.

"It was a long drive," the Earl said, "and as I intend to win your Steeple-Chase tomorrow, I must have some sleep!"

"There will be plenty of time for that," Imogen said softly.

As she spoke she raised her arms above her shoulders.

Very slowly with the softness of a sigh, her nightgown fell to the ground . . .

After that there had been no need for words.

The Earl thought now he had never known her so insatiably passionate.

He opened his eyes and realised it was still dark.

The candle which had gutted low gave no more than a flicker of light.

Imogen raised her head from his shoulder.

"I must leave you, Darol," she said, "and there will be no need for hurry first thing in the morning because we are not being married until noon!"

The Earl drew in his breath.

He felt he could not have heard her aright.

"What – did you say?"

"The Steeple-Chase can wait," Imogen replied. "I have arranged instead, my wonderful, adorable lover, that we will be married in my private Chapel and our friends are all very excited at the idea!"

It flashed through the Earl's mind that that was the reason why they had been looking at him strangely.

Why it had been so difficult to talk to them about the Steeple-Chase.

Aloud he said;

"I must be very stupid in misunderstanding what you are saying to me, Imogen. I have always made it quite clear that I have no intention of marrying anyone for a long time yet!"

"You are going to marry me!" Imogen insisted. "And I know we shall be very happy."

"When I marry," the Earl said firmly, "I will do my own proposing and make my own arrangements."

"That is what I would have liked you to do," Imogen answered, "but you have been somewhat reluctant, my dearest, to say the words I have been waiting to hear. So I decided to speed things up a little."

"I am sorry to disappoint you," the Earl said, "but now that you have done the proposing, my answer to your invitation is 'No'!"

Imogen gave a little laugh.

"Do you really think I would accept 'No', as an answer?" she enquired. "Suppose I told you I am having a baby?"

"I would not believe it and could only reply that it is a lie."

Vaguely at the back of his mind the Earl remembered hearing why she had not given Basset a child.

It had not interested him particularly at the time.

Imogen, it was said, had been made barren by a riding accident which she had had when she was young.

Anyway, it was something that had never entered his head while he had been involved with her.

"If I am not having one now," Imogen said lightly, "then I will have one as soon as we are married because of course, I realise that you need an heir."

The way she spoke was too glib.

The Earl was quite certain he was right in thinking that a child was an impossibility.

"Baby, or no baby," he replied, "I am not going to marry you, Imogen!"

"That is where you are mistaken," she replied. "Everything is arranged and if you have to be *persuaded* up the aisle, my two brothers are only too eager to do the persuading."

The way she spoke was a threat and the Earl realised exactly what she meant.

Her brothers would be delighted to be in a position in which he would be obliged to settle their debts in order to avoid a scandal.

He could imagine nothing more humiliating than being frog-marched into the Chapel with one of them on either side of him.

Imogen bent forward unexpectedly and kissed him lightly on the lips.

"Stop trying to escape the inevitable," she said. "As I have already told you, we will be very happy, and I shall enjoy more than I have ever enjoyed anything in my life being the Countess of Kelvindale!"

As she finished speaking she got out of bed.

Picking up her nightgown from the floor she slipped it over her head.

She then stood for a moment looking down at the Earl.

He was staring at her as if he found it hard to believe she was real.

Then she walked towards the door.

"Sleep well, my darling!" she said. "You will understand that I am locking you in to prevent you from trying to escape. I promise you I shall make a very beautiful Bride!"

She left the room and the Earl heard the key being turned in the lock.

For a moment it was impossible to move.

Then he told himself that somehow, although he was not certain how, he must escape this trap that had been set for him.

He now realised how skilful it was.

Among the guests he noticed that Imogen had included two professional gossip-mongers who would make the most of the story.

There was also a man whom he remembered as being an eminent and very popular Lawyer.

He was there to ensure that he signed a Marriage Settlement.

It would undoubtedly make Imogen secure for the rest of her life whether they were together or separated.

"She has thought of everything!" he exclaimed furiously.

He got out of bed and going to the door found it was, as he anticipated, made of stout oak.

Without tools it would be impossible to break it open.

He then went to the window and understood why he had been given this particular room.

It was on the west side of the house and there

was no balcony but a sheer drop into the garden below.

If he tried to escape that way it would mean inevitably a broken leg or worse.

There was no dressing-room with a connecting door, and the chimney was too narrow for him to attempt to climb it.

He swore however he would not be defeated.

He dressed himself quickly in his riding-clothes.

It was with an expertise that always annoyed his valet who disliked his being so self-sufficient.

First he looked around the room, then he pulled the sheets from the bed, but there were only two of them.

He looked at the curtains.

They were not made of velvet, but of a more pliable silk.

He pulled them down and knotted them to the sheets by reef-knots.

His father had taught him how to tie these when he was a small boy.

His make-shift rope was not however long enough and he was obliged to add the blankets to it.

There were fortunately four of them.

He reckoned now there was nearly enough rope for him to reach the ground safely.

He tied the sheet forming one end of the rope round the thick wooden leg of the four-poster bed.

He knew it would take a great deal more than his weight to shift it even a few inches across the floor.

He opened the window as wide as it would go and realised as he did so that the stars were fading.

In a short while there would be the hush before the dawn.

Then would come the first fingers of light over the horizon.

He threw his make-shift rope out through the window and knew he had not been mistaken in thinking it would serve his purpose.

He put on his high cravat and after that his cut-away riding-coat.

He filled his pocket with all the money he had brought with him.

He prayed that his self-made mode of escape would not fail him.

If it did he would go crashing to the ground below.

He was not certain because it was difficult to see in the darkness, but he thought there was a flower-bed immediately underneath.

He hoped he was not mistaken.

He turned to look back into the bedroom.

As he did so the candle by the bed gave one last despairing flicker and went out.

With a slight twist of his lips the Earl hoped it was not an omen of what would happen to him.

To make quite sure he tested the sheet that was round the leg of the bed.

He made sure the knot he had tied tightly would hold.

Slowly he climbed out of the window and down the side of the house.

He had fortunately learnt about mountaineering from his father.

As a boy he had climbed mountains in Wales, when they were staying with a relative.

To his great delight he had reached the top.

He had always been determined that when he had time he would visit Switzerland and climb the Alps.

This he had not done to date.

But he still remembered how to use a rope and how to keep his feet steady on the brick wall of the house.

When the rope ended he had to drop the last six feet.

He did so and was relieved to find he had been right in surmising there was a flower-bed beneath his window.

He landed in it and it broke the shock of his drop.

Then as swiftly as he could without making a noise about it he hurried to the stables.

There was only one sleepy young groom on duty in the main stable where his horses had been put.

The lad looked up in astonishment as the Earl said:

"It may seem a little early, but as I am unable to sleep I wish to ride one of my horses."

The boy scrambled up from the hay on which he had been sleeping.

He followed the Earl who had moved to the stall where he could see his stallion by the light of a lantern.

It was the horse on which he had intended to win the Steeple-Chase.

He thought it was exactly what he wanted for his escape.

Because the stable-lad was still rather drowsy he helped him saddle *Jupiter*, and as he tightened the girths he said;

"I am the Earl of Kelvindale. Tell my Head Groom when he wakes to take my Travelling-Chariot with my other horses back home immediately!"

He repeated the message to be quite sure the boy understood.

He then gave him a sovereign which he grasped excitedly.

The Earl then led *Jupiter* out into the yard.

He mounted quickly, afraid that if he did not hurry Imogen might think of some way of preventing him from getting away.

She might even send her brothers or the servants after him.

He rode away in a direction on which he would not be seen from the house and told himself that he had managed to evade her.

He realised however that he still had to cover a great many miles before he could feel safe.

He knew Imogen well enough now to know there was beneath her beauty a stone-hard determination.

It would make her hang on to him tenaciously.

She had decided to marry him, and he knew now that nothing she could do would be too low, too mean, or too unpleasant if it ensured her becoming his wife.

"I have to be intelligent about this," the Earl thought as he reached some level ground and gave *Jupiter* his head.

He intended to make his way back to his own house, Kelvin Priory, and it would be a long and difficult journey across country.

Kelvin Priory was one of the finest and most magnificent ancestral homes in the whole of England.

The estate had been in the hands of the family since the 12th century.

It was built at the same time as the first Earl of Kelvindale had been created.

The Earl was exceedingly proud of it as he was proud of his lineage.

He had never in his wildest dreams thought of putting Imogen in his mother's place as the Countess of Kelvindale.

He had adored his mother who had died when he was at Oxford.

It still hurt him to think he had lost her.

She occupied, although he had never spoken of it, a special shrine in his heart.

He vaguely thought it would one day be filled by his wife.

It would be unthinkable that someone promiscuous and in many ways as outrageous as Imogen should take any part in his life except as his mistress.

"How can I have been so idiotic," the Earl asked himself now, "not to have guessed that as a widow she would want to marry me?"

The other Beauties with whom he had had ardent *affaires de coeur* had had complacent husbands who pretended to be unaware of what was happening.

They accepted that the Earl was a noted marksman, and said they preferred to be in the country rather than London.

The Earl was remembering now innumerable occasions when what Imogen said should have alerted him to what she was planning.

It seemed to him now utterly and completely impossible that like some 'Greenhorn' he had walked into the trap she had prepared for him.

"It is something that will never happen again!" he promised himself.

At the same time, he knew he had still to make sure that he was not recaptured.

Jupiter was undoubtedly faster than any of the horses that Imogen owned.

There were however two men in the party who, the Earl thought, might catch up with him.

Besides of course, the grooms or the out-riders.

They could borrow horses from the other guests who had brought fine horse-flesh with them.

"It never occurred to me," the Earl murmured with a flash of humour, "that what was arranged was not a Steeple-Chase, but a hunt! And I was the quarry!"

The mere thought of it made him spur *Jupiter* on.

He rode until he realised it was nearly midday.

He was wondering if he dared call at any of the local Inns.

The danger was they could be questioned later and would be able to describe him accurately.

Then he told himself it was a risk he must take.

He therefore stopped at the next village.

It was a small one with just a few thatched cottages, a Norman Church and a black-and-white Inn.

The latter was on the village green which also sported the stocks.

There appeared to be no one about.

The Earl rode *Jupiter* into a small yard where he saw there was a thatched, rather rough stable which was empty.

He led *Jupiter* inside and found some fresh hay in the manger.

He filled an empty bucket with water from an adjacent pump.

He then walked into the Inn to find it was kept by a very old man.

He looked at him questioningly with eyes which the Earl suspected were nearly blind.

He asked for something to eat and was told there was some cold ham and ripe cheese, but nothing else.

He quickly replied that that was all he required, and ordered at the same time a mug of home-brewed cider.

He ate and drank quickly.

Having paid for what he received he asked the old man where he was.

It took him some time to understand.

But he thought he was going in the right direction which would eventually lead him home.

He left the Inn.

Remounting *Jupiter* who appeared to have enjoyed the rest, the Earl set off again.

Three hours later he told himself that he was lost.

He would have to ask the way from the next person he saw.

As he had kept to the fields and only crossed the main roads without travelling on them he had come across very few pedestrians.

He thought that if he was to be home before dark he would have to hurry.

He was moving across a flat grassy field.

There were some sheep at the far end of it.

He was half-way across when he realised that ahead of him there was a high hedge.

He would have to jump it unless he was to turn back towards the gate which was apparently the only way out.

The hedge would be no difficulty where *Jupiter* was concerned.

The Earl rode him at it and lifted him up with his usual expertise.

Only as they swept over with many inches to spare he realised to his dismay that there was a deep pit on the other side.

Around it were scattered a number of large stones.

Jupiter recognised the danger at the same time as his master.

He stretched out as far as he could, but he stumbled against the far edge of the pit.

The Earl was thrown over his head.

Shaken the stallion staggered to his feet, but the Earl lay still.

CHAPTER TWO

Carita heard a loud voice in the hall and shuddered.

She knew that her Stepfather had returned and she felt the usual little tremor of fear run through her.

Ever since her Mother had died her Stepfather, Sir Mortimer Haldon, had become even more aggressive and more domineering than he had been before.

She had hated him from the first moment that he had married her Mother.

At the same time, she could understand why her beautiful, gentle, sweet, rather ineffective Mother had accepted him.

It was impossible for Mary Wensley to live without a man to look after her.

She had married her handsome dashing husband, who had swept her off her feet, when she was very young.

Despite her family's opposition they had been married a month after they met each other.

One of the reasons was that Richard Wensley was a naval officer and was never certain when his ship would have to join the Fleet or when he would return.

By great good fortune, he spent the first two years of their marriage in a shore job at Portsmouth.

It was found he was so clever with the young seamen

and such a good organiser that the authorities had done everything they could to keep him employed on land.

Finally after two years the War had been won and Richard went to sea again.

He was posted to the West Indies from where he never returned.

It was then that his wife collapsed.

Nothing Carita said or did could make any difference to her Mother's utter despair at having lost the man she loved.

Because she was intelligent Carita understood that one of the things which endeared her Mother to her Father was that she was completely dependent on him.

He himself had a very strong character which she hoped she herself had in part inherited.

He liked to be master in his own home, and to feel it was his protection and love that kept his wife happy.

Six months passed before belatedly the news came back to England that he had died.

Not in battle, but from some tropical fever.

Mary Wensley had almost cried herself into the grave.

Then unexpectedly when she and Carita were still living in the small rented house in Portsmouth Sir Mortimer Haldon made their acquaintance.

Carita could not remember afterwards where they met him.

Yet suddenly he was filling the small house with his overwhelming presence.

Because he was so dominating Mary Wensley turned to him as if he was an elixir which brought her back to life.

Carita had been fifteen at the time.

Sir Mortimer seemed to her in every possible way different from her Father, whom she had adored.

She shrank from him, and he was aware of her feelings.

Once he had married her Mother she became a challenge which he found it impossible to resist.

He tried at first to gain her affection, or at least her gratitude, by honeyed words and small gifts.

She had to admit that he was generous to her Mother and was prepared to be generous to her.

But some intuition within herself told her he was not what he pretended to be.

That he was in fact an evil man.

She could not explain why she thought this, and yet the feeling was undoubtedly there.

Mary Wensley did not take long in making up her mind to marry Sir Mortimer.

Or rather, he made it up for her, and things changed dramatically.

Sir Mortimer moved them from Portsmouth to his large, ugly house in Oxfordshire.

As they drove down the drive towards it Carita thought it was as unpleasant-looking as its owner.

Inside it was over-luxurious and over-furnished.

She longed for the small dilapidated house they had lived in with her Father.

She knew, however, and she tried to be glad, that her Mother, if not wildly in love with her second husband, was content.

She was petted, cosseted and surrounded with everything she could possibly desire.

Gowns, furs and jewellery were heaped upon her.

Sir Mortimer played the part of the infatuated admirer which deceived everybody who came to see them.

It was only Carita who realised there was a definitely boastful note in his voice when he explained to his friends:

"My dear wife was the daughter of Lord Murcot, and she was married to Captain the Honourable Richard Wensley, who unfortunately lost his life while serving with His Majesty's Navy."

"It is all a feather in *his* cap!" Carita told herself scornfully.

There as she met her Stepfather's eyes across the room she had the uncomfortable feeling that he could read her thoughts.

She tried for her Mother's sake to be polite, and of course, grateful for what he gave her.

But she knew as the years passed that he expected her to go down on her knees when she thanked him for a new gown.

"Mortimer tells me," her mother would say, "that you were not grateful for the fur muff he gave you. Surely, dearest, you realise how kind he is?"

"Yes, of course, Mama, but I did say thank you."

"Not fervently enough, dearest," her mother would say. "Please try to assure him that you are pleased with what he gives you."

Carita tried, but she knew that all her Stepfather's gifts had an ulterior motive.

They were intended to hurt and humiliate her, and that included the fur muff.

He gave her that just after she had lost the tabby cat which had been her constant companion ever since she had come to Haldon Hall.

She was certain that it was deliberate that the fur of the muff was exactly the colour of her beloved cat.

It might have been coincidence but the same sort of thing had happened a dozen times over.

A gown purchased in London would arrive and it would be green.

That was a colour about which she was superstitious.

Her Father had also believed it to be unlucky.

There were innumerable little pin-pricks.

She told herself she should be too big to notice them.

Yet they were there.

On one terrifying occasion when she was sixteen, Sir Mortimer had lost his temper and beaten her.

It was a humiliation she did not wish to think about.

She had gone to her Mother saying she must leave the Hall immediately.

Her Mother held her closely in her arms and for the first time defied her husband.

"If you touch Carita again," she warned him when they were alone, "I will leave you."

"What are you saying to me?" Sir Mortimer asked gruffly.

"Carita is Richard's child, not yours. She may be difficult, as all girls are at that age, but I will not have her physically assaulted by anyone!"

It was the first time Mary had ever stood up to him.

He was wise enough to put his arms around her and promise it would never happen again.

He had left Carita with the idea however that he had beaten her not only for what she had done, but also because he enjoyed doing it.

From that moment he had tried all the more to humiliate her in every way possible.

He would laugh mockingly at almost everything she said.

If it was possible to hold her up to ridicule to his friends when her mother was not there, he did so.

She did all she could to keep out of the way.

She began to think it would be better if she went to stay with one of her Mother's relatives.

It would however, be a difficult thing to do because she had not seen any of them for years.

In the first place they none of them had lived near Portsmouth.

Secondly when they occasionally wrote to her Mother she was sure they did not approve of Sir Mortimer.

One day, after he had been particularly offensive to her, she had said to her Mother:

"Would it not be best, Mama, if I asked Aunt Elizabeth if I might go to stay with her in Yorkshire? Perhaps until I am old enough not to require Governesses and teachers."

Her mother had given a cry of horror.

"You know, darling, I cannot lose you!"

She held out her arms and there were tears in her eyes as she said:

"You are all I have left of darling Richard. When I look at you I can see him as if he was standing beside me, and I know that I have not lost him completely."

The tears had run down her Mother's cheeks.

Carita had wiped them away promising that she would never leave her.

Then six months ago, quite unexpectedly, her Mother had died.

She had not been well during the winter and had suffered from one heavy cold after another.

They left her limp and listless.

She made every effort when Sir Mortimer was present to appear animated and attentive.

But as soon as he had gone riding or was engaged with his friends, she seemed to collapse.

She would just lie with closed eyes, not asleep, but as if in her thoughts she had moved into another world.

One day Sir Mortimer had said that he had to attend a dinner.

It was being given by the Lord Lieutenant for the more important Landowners in the county.

"It is 'Men Only', my dear," he had said to his wife, "which means, I am afraid, that you cannot accompany me."

"I am sure that everyone will be very happy to have you there," Carita heard her Mother say.

She spoke in the soft admiring voice she always used when speaking to Sir Mortimer.

She knew it pleased him.

He seemed to swell a little with pride as he answered:

"I have prepared an excellent speech, making a few suggestions for the future which I am sure will gain the approval of the Lord Lieutenant."

"I am sure they will!" his wife said.

When he had gone out, looking, Carita thought, fat, pompous and somewhat over-dressed in his evening-clothes, her Mother was too tired to move.

"I will have dinner with you in your bedroom," Carita said. "It is far too much for you to get up and come downstairs."

"That will be lovely, darling," her Mother managed to murmur.

When dinner came it was very appetising, but she did not want anything to eat.

Because she seemed so fragile Carita was alarmed

and tried to persuade her to have a glass of champagne.

"I am sure it would be better for you, Mama, than those nasty medicines the Doctor has given you."

"They make me feel worse," her Mother replied, "but I really want nothing."

She had a few sips however.

The dinner-tray was then taken away and Carita sat down beside the bed and took her Mother's hand in hers.

"I am worried about you, Mama."

"There is nothing to worry about," her mother answered. "Last night I dreamt of your father and he was very near me."

Carita's fingers tightened on hers.

Her mother was speaking in a way she had not heard her speaking before.

"Darling . . Richard," she murmured, "I have missed him . . I have missed him . . so terribly . . now he has . . come for me . . and we will be . . together again . ."

Carita gasped.

Then before she could say anything, as she went down on her knees beside her mother's bed, she heard her say:

"Oh . . Richard . . Richard! You are here . . I have been . . so . . miserable without . . you."

There was a new and rapt note in her voice.

Her eyes were open and there was a dazzling radiance in her face.

It made her look younger and lovelier than Carita had seen her look for years.

Just for a moment everything seemed to stand still.

Then her mother's eyes closed.

Carita had known before she touched her that she was dead, or rather that she had gone with her father where they could be together.

There was no doubt that Sir Mortimer was genuinely upset by his wife's death.

He had in fact loved her in his own way.

But there was no one else to whom he could express his feelings, and he therefore raged at Carita.

"Why the hell did you not tell me that your Mother was so ill?" he asked furiously. "You must have known – you must have had some idea that she was dying."

"Of course I had no idea of it!" Carita retorted. "But if she had to die, then I think it was the way she would have wished to go."

She did not say that her Father had come for her Mother.

Or that to witness her end had been a wonderful experience which she would never forget.

As if he suspected something of the sort, Sir Mortimer questioned her over and over again.

What had her Mother said? What had happened? How had she died and how had she finally stopped breathing?

"Did she speak? Did she mention me?" he asked.

"No, Step-papa!"

"I cannot believe that is true," Sir Mortimer said angrily.

None of her Mother's relations came to the Funeral.

Carita had in fact written to them to tell them when it was taking place.

But the journey was either too long, or in the case of some of the elderly cousins they had not seen Mary for years.

So a letter of condolence had to suffice.

Of course Sir Mortimer insisted on a very big and solemn Funeral.

Because he was of some importance in the County, a great number of people who hardly knew his wife attended the Service.

There were also his particular friends with whom he went hunting.

Of course they all came back to an elaborate luncheon at The Hall afterwards.

Carita did not go into the Dining-Room.

Because there was a great deal not only to eat but also to drink, she could hear their voices.

They were growing louder and louder.

When finally the guests left they made a tremendous amount of noise as they went to the front door.

She would have remained in her bedroom had her Step-father not sent for her.

She had come downstairs, her face very pale, her eyes swollen because she had cried bitterly after the Funeral was over.

"You are to keep me company," he said roughly. "I have no wish to sit alone brooding because your Mother is no longer with me."

Obediently she dined with him, but she found it an ordeal.

He talked incessantly of how generous he had been to her Mother and to her.

He went over all he had done for them since he had come to what he called 'that little pig-sty of a house' in Portsmouth.

"What would your Mother have done if I had not taken pity on her," he asked, "and brought her here where she could have every comfort and everything she desired?"

He paused before he added:

"And that goes for you, too, although God knows you are damned ungrateful."

"I am grateful, Step-papa," Carita expostulated, "and I have always thanked you for everything you have ever given me."

"Yes, thanked me with your lips and cursed me with your eyes!" Sir Mortimer roared. "Do you suppose I do not know what you feel about me?"

He paused before he went on:

"I am not so insensitive that I am deceived by the lip-service your Mother told you to pay me!"

"I am sorry if I upset you, Step-papa," Carita said, "but I think, now that Mama is no longer with us, it would be best if I went away and lived with one of my own relatives if they will have me."

"And have everybody saying I have thrust you back into the gutter from which I rescued you?" Sir Mortimer roared. "You will stay here with me and at least there will be somebody in the house for me to talk to when I come home in the evening!"

Carita made an effort to be as pleasant to him as she could.

After all, she told herself, he must be suffering at the loss of her Mother as much as she was.

If it was anything like the agony she was feeling, she should be sorry for him.

Within a week of her Mother's death, however, the men whom Sir Mortimer called his friends were there lunching, dining and drinking.

It was as if they now had a right to be at The Hall which had not been accorded to them before.

This Carita knew to be the truth.

It was her Mother who had said that she would not

entertain certain of her Stepfather's friends of whom she disapproved.

They were all hard-drinking, somewhat common men, Carita thought, with whom he had spent a great deal of his time before he had remarried.

It was only when he began to try to raise himself socially in the County that he had dropped these men.

She was sure it was they who earned for him such a bad reputation in the past.

Sir Mortimer had been married before, but his wife had been of no importance.

He had been a widower for over ten years when he had met her Mother.

It was not only because he found her Mother attractive that she meant so much to him.

It was also because with her as his wife he had been able to make an effort to play a part in the County that he had never played before.

Thinking back, Carita could hear the satisfaction in his voice when he had said to her mother:

"The Lord Lieutenant spoke to me today. He was very gracious and asked, my dear, after your health."

Another time he said:

"I have doubled my subscription to the Hunt, and the Master who you know is Lord Grameton, thanked me. I feel sure, my dear, we shall be invited to dine with him before the Hunt Ball in November."

Carita could understand now what she had been too young to realise at the time.

Her Mother had been a ladder up which her Step-father had climbed higher and higher every year.

"Mama would have had no idea of it," she thought gratefully. "She never suspected that people had ulterior motives for what they did, and I am glad I did not mention it to her."

Every day Carita found life at the Hall becoming more and more unpleasant.

Her Stepfather started to entertain apart from his drinking cronies, but they were all people she had never met before.

She had the suspicion they had just been waiting for her Mother to die.

Then they could all come creeping back to partake of her Stepfather's hospitality, especially the wines that came from his large and well-stocked cellar.

Because they drank so much she would slip away the moment dinner was over.

She would lock herself in her bedroom.

She thought there was something degrading about the men with bloated, red and sweating faces.

The women laughed too shrilly and flirted in a manner that would have shocked her Mother.

"I must talk to Step-papa again," she thought now as she heard him coming down the corridor towards the library.

It was a large room and when she was alone it was a relief to be able to read and forget her surroundings.

She could forget the men who paid her embarrassing compliments and behaved with other women in a manner which she thought degrading.

She hoped her Stepfather would go into his study which was next door to the library.

Instead he opened the door of the library and exclaimed;

"There you are! I thought you would be here ruining your eyes with all that reading when you should have been out in the fresh air."

He was just finding fault for the sake of doing so.

Carita put down her book and rose to her feet.

"I went riding on *Mercury* this afternoon, Step-papa," she said, "and it was such a lovely day and not too hot, even though it is the end of July."

Her Stepfather did not answer.

He merely walked into the room to stand in front of the mantelpiece, as he usually did.

"I want to talk to you, Carita."

She moved nearer to him and sat down on one of the armchairs.

He was looking, she thought, particularly unpleasant.

His stock was crumpled at his neck and several buttons of his waist-coat were undone.

She suspected he had been drinking with one of his cronies.

His face was flushed and his hair, what was left of it, was untidy.

She waited.

After a moment he asked:

"Are you listening to me?"

"Yes . . of course, Step-papa."

"Then I can tell you that you are an extremely lucky girl – very lucky indeed!"

Carita raised her eye-brows.

"In what way?" she enquired.

"I have just been over to visit Lord Stilbury. He had said he wanted to speak to me on an important matter, so I rode over to see him."

"It must be five miles over to Stilbury House," Carita remarked.

Her Stepfather did not answer.

He was staring at her in a way she most disliked.

It was a manner which recently had made her shudder.

While she could not quite understand it, she thought that almost despite himself, he admired her.

She knew she resembled her Mother.

At the same time there was something strange and rather unpleasant in the way he regarded her.

Now he looked at her for so long that at last she said:

"What is it, Step-papa? Has anything upset you?"

"Upset me?" he replied. "No, of course not! I am delighted – absolutely delighted with what Stilbury said to me. I suppose you are curious to know what it is?"

"Y.yes . . of course," Carita said because it was expected of her.

"God knows, I never expected anything like it," Sir Mortimer went on, "but Stilbury, my dear Stepdaughter, has asked for your hand in Marriage!"

Carita gave a little gasp.

"You . . you cannot be serious!"

"Serious? Of course I am serious!" Sir Mortimer roared. "And while I admit it has taken me by surprise, I am honoured – deeply honoured – to think that you will take such an important position in the County. In fact, second only to the Lord Lieutenant's wife, and Stilbury will, to all intents and purposes, be my son-in-law."

Carita could understand that but Lord Stilbury was as old, if not older, than her Stepfather.

She remembered now he had been at dinner two nights ago and more than once the week before.

She had thought him one of the most unattractive and unpleasant of her Stepfather's friends.

He was a large man, tall and heavily built, but his face was long and thin.

Now she thought about it, his lips were cruel and in keeping with his reputation.

She could not remember who had talked about him to her.

She thought it must have been one of the women of whom her Mother would not have approved.

"He is a cold man for whom I have no liking," the woman had said, "and I can well believe all the stories of how he ill-treated his wife, beating her to death, so rumour has it!"

"I do not believe that!" another woman said. "But I have heard that he is hard on his horses and his stable-boys are terrified of him!"

The conversation came back to her although she had not thought of it before.

Quickly, not even thinking of what she should say, she cried out;

"No . . of course I could . . not marry . . Lord Stilbury! He is . . horrible and far . . far too . . old!"

"Do you know what you are saying?" Sir Mortimer enquired. "Stilbury is one of the most important men in Oxfordshire! He is very rich and his house and estate are larger than mine!"

"I am not interested in what he possesses," Carita protested. "But how could I marry a man who is old enough to be my Grandfather, and who it is said was so . . cruel to his wife that she . . died from the . . way he . . ill-treated her!"

"Gossip! who listens to gossip but silly little chits like you?" Sir Mortimer shouted. "How dare you, a girl without a penny to your name, turn down a man who is so distinguished and so rich that you will never want for anything for the rest of your life?"

"I do not want his money or position," Carita

retorted. "When I marry, which I hope I shall do
. . one day, I want to be in love . . as my Mother . .
loved my . . Father."

Even as she spoke she knew she had said the wrong
thing.

"And what did loving your Father get her?" Sir
Mortimer asked. "A rented house in Portsmouth which,
as I have said before, was no bigger than a pig-sty."

"But we were . . happy there," Carita flashed.

"Happy?" Sir Mortimer snorted. "With you and your
Mother half in rags, not enough food to keep a chicken
alive, and with no hope for the future but – penury?"

He was working himself into a rage as he went on:

"Penury – yes, that is the right word – penury!"

He shouted it at her and Carita rose to her feet.

"You may sneer at the house in which we lived with
my Father when he was not at sea," Carita said quietly,
"but we were very, very . . happy."

"Then you are even more half-witted than I thought!"
Sir Mortimer said. "Perhaps you do not realise that
it is a life to which you can return if you refuse
the amazing offer that has been made to you by
Stilbury!"

"That is what I intend to do," Carita said quietly,
"so, will you please tell him, Step-papa, that while I
am deeply . . honoured by his . . offer, my answer is
. . 'No'!"

Sir Mortimer stared at her.

Then he threw back his head and laughed a loud and
raucous laugh that had no humour in it.

"Do you really believe, you stupid little fool," he said,
"that I would allow you to refuse a man like Stilbury?
You will accept him and thank God on your knees for
being made such an offer."

Once again he was working himself up into a rage as he went on:

"What have you got to attract a man except a pretty face? You are penniless – do you understand that? – you are completely penniless except for what I give you."

His voice grew louder as he went on:

"Stilbury, God help him, is infatuated with you! And Heaven knows, I am not going to enlighten him as to what a tiresome, ungrateful little Brat you are!"

Carita turned as if she would leave the room, but Sir Mortimer roared:

"You will stay here and listen to what I have to say! Let me make it clear once and for all – I have accepted Stilbury's offer and he is calling on you tomorrow to set the date for the wedding!"

"I will . . not marry him . . Step-papa, I will . . not!" Carita cried. "I think he is . . revolting and I have . . no wish to . . die as his first wife . . did through his . . cruelty!"

"If that is what you are afraid of," Sir Mortimer sneered, "then I know how to deal with you my girl! Let me make one thing clear . ."

He pointed a thick finger at her as he said:

"If you refuse to accept Stilbury tomorrow, I will beat you every day until you do! Make no mistake, if I have to carry you semi-conscious to the altar, that is what I shall do!"

He was drawing nearer to her as he spoke.

With a sudden cry of horror Carita turned and ran from the room before he could stop her.

She slammed the door behind her.

Then she was running down the corridor which led to the hall and up the stairs.

Running into her bedroom she closed the door and locked it.

Then she flung herself down on the bed and buried her face in her pillows.

It could not be true!

What she had just been told must be some ghastly nightmare from which she would wake up.

How could she possibly marry a man who was so old?

Now she thought about it, she was certain he was as wicked and cruel as she had heard he was.

Although her Stepfather made her shudder, she knew that what she would feel for Lord Stilbury was even worse.

It came back to her now that when he had shaken hands with her each time he came to the house she had felt a revulsion.

His hand was cold and clammy, and there had been something about him from which she instinctively shrank.

"Oh . . Mama . . save me!" she murmured. "Save me . . save me! How can I . . possibly live . . with a man I . . loathe?"

She thought of how he had beaten his wife and been cruel to his horses.

Then she remembered what her Stepfather had threatened.

After he had beaten her before, he had promised her Mother he would never touch her again.

But her Mother was no longer there.

In his anxiety to be connected by marriage with Lord Stilbury, she was quite certain he would not only beat her, but enjoy doing it.

She knew only too well that flicker in his eyes when he humiliated her in one way or another.

Nothing could be more humiliating or degrading than to be beaten by him.

Yet it was what he would undoubtedly do, until he got his own way.

"I cannot . . bear it! Oh . . God . . I cannot . . bear it!" she murmured.

She thought of her Father and the radiance in her Mother's face as she had died.

It was then, almost as if her Father was talking to her and guiding her, that she knew what she must do.

She wondered why she had not thought of it before.

Slowly she rose from the bed.

She would run away and she would have to leave before Lord Stilbury called tomorrow afternoon.

She walked across the room to stand at the window looking out.

The heat of the day had gone and now the shadows were growing longer.

The birds were going to roost.

Everything seemed very quiet and unchanging, except that her own world had turned topsy-turvy and had crashed about her ears.

"What . . can I do . . where can . . I go?" she asked and waited for an answer.

It was then, again, as if her Father was telling her, that she remembered that he had a brother who lived in Norfolk.

He was apparently a strange man, older than her father.

According to what she had been told, her Uncle lived alone and in seclusion, preferring the company of animals to people.

He wrote about them.

Books and articles for those who were interested in breeding the best cattle, the finest sheep, and dogs of breeds that were not usually to be found in England.

Carita could remember pleading when she was a little girl:

"Do tell me about him, Papa."

"He is much older than I am," her Father had said, "and happy in his own peculiar way. He has no wish to go to parties, or to meet people, unless they share the same interests as himself."

"He sounds a very strange man, Papa," Carita had said.

"All men have different interests," her Father had explained. "I love the sea, and I always wanted to be a sailor. My brother, Andrew, even when he was very young, was what one might call a 'Loner'!

He paused a moment before continuing:

"When he was left a little money by his Godfather, he moved off on his own and I very seldom hear from him."

Andrew had however written to her Mother when her father's death was reported in the newspapers.

A kind letter if a somewhat impersonal one.

Carita knew now that this was where she must hide.

Perhaps Uncle Andrew would think of her as a 'lost sheep' and protect her.

"That is where I will go!" she told herself.

She tried to be practical and think logically of what she should do.

Later there was a knock on the door.

When she asked who it was, a footman replied:

"The Master says 'e expects you down to dinner, Miss Carita."

"Tell him I have a headache and have retired to bed," Carita replied.

The footman went away and she started packing.

She knew it would be difficult to take much with her.

She therefore chose three light muslin gowns which would take up very little room, a nightgown and a few underclothes.

She knew they could all be packed into the bag attached to *Mercury*'s saddle.

She would wear her best riding-habit, and when winter came she would have to buy a coat.

The thought of buying anything reminded her that she would want money.

She realised she had very little because there had been no need of it.

Sir Mortimer had been generous to her Mother and paid every bill without complaint, even from the most expensive shops in Bond Street.

Carita had a few silver coins to put on the plate in Church.

She occasionally bought a glass of cider when she was out riding.

Otherwise she had not required ready money.

"I must have some now . . I must!" she thought.

It was a long way to Norfolk and she would have to stop on the way and stable *Mercury*.

He must have proper oats to eat, and she had no wish herself to go hungry.

It was then she remembered her Mother's jewellery.

The most valuable pieces were downstairs in the safe and she could not get them.

But the jewellery her Mother wore during the day and on ordinary occasions was in her jewel-case.

48

She wore jewellery every day because it pleased her husband.

It also contained brooches, bracelets, necklaces and earrings which as Lady Haldon she had worn whenever they had a special party.

"I will take Mama's things with me," Carita decided.

She was wise enough to know it would be a mistake to put them into her saddle-bag.

She might have to let grooms or other servants in the Inns carry it for her.

She had been warned by her Mother whenever they were travelling to be very careful of thieves.

She therefore hid the brooches inside the lining of her riding-coat.

While they might be uncomfortable, at least they would be safe.

Then as she looked at her Mother's jewel-case she had an idea.

It contained her Mother's wedding-ring which her Father had given her.

She had removed it when Sir Mortimer bought her his.

Carita slipped the ring onto her finger and found that it fitted her perfectly.

She thought as she did so that once again her Father was telling her what to do.

As a young girl it would be considered reprehensible for her to travel without a chaperone.

A married woman however could ride through the country with only a groom keeping his distance.

If she had to stop somewhere she could always say that her groom's horse had lost a shoe.

He would therefore be joining her later.

If she was wearing a wedding-ring they would not

question for a moment that she was not what she pretended to be.

To make certain she added to it one of her Mother's diamond rings.

She was, however, still afraid she might need money if her Uncle refused to shelter her.

After thinking for some minutes she sewed a diamond bracelet which she knew was valuable into the hem of her riding-skirt.

She fixed it securely in a place where it would not rub against her legs.

She had another which was narrower in the back of her riding-jacket.

"I have been clever, very clever!" she thought as she finished her task.

She put everything ready including her ankle-boots and her riding-hat, then she undressed.

She prayed for a long time before she got into bed: that her Father would help her and that God would protect her.

Finally she lay down feeling calmer.

. . . .

It was still dark as Carita crept down the stairs.

She let herself out at the nearest door that led to the stables.

When she reached them there was only one elderly groom on duty.

He was sitting in the Harness-Room in a wooden armchair with his feet on another, fast asleep.

Carita did not disturb him, but tip-toed away to the stall where *Mercury* was resting and saddled him herself.

He nuzzled against her as he always did.

She had thought since her Mother had died that *Mercury* was the only real friend she had left.

She led him out into the yard and he waited while she climbed onto the mounting-block, then onto his back.

Moving slowly so that she made little noise, she left the stables by the back gate which led into the open countryside.

She had a fair idea in which direction she had to go.

She was determined to ride across country and she knew she must quickly put as much distance between herself and The Hall as possible.

When her Stepfather realised she was missing, he would organise a search for her.

She went fast, but was careful not to over-tire *Mercury*.

He had been her special mount ever since she had come to The Hall.

If she was not grateful for anything else her Stepfather had given her, she had thanked him sincerely for *Mercury*.

She rode on, not stopping except to let *Mercury* drink from a clear stream which they crossed and which came only up to his fetlocks.

Then they went on again.

Now Carita was beginning to wonder where she could find somewhere to stay for the night.

She had ready her story about her 'groom' who was to follow her.

She was looking for a quiet little Inn where they would not ask too many questions.

Wherever it was, it must be somewhere where it was unlikely her Stepfather would make enquiries.

She was quite certain he would search for her because

he would be determined, whatever she said, that she should marry Lord Stilbury.

She saw a field ahead where she thought men must have been working during the day.

There were marks of cart-wheels on the grass.

She could see that on one side of it there was a deep pit in which they must have been digging.

She was wondering why, when suddenly, over the high hedge which stood behind the pit, came a horse.

It jumped superbly and she thought at first it would be able to clear the pit although it extended some way beyond the ledges.

Then she saw the horse stumble on the very lip of the pit.

She gave a cry of horror as the man riding him was thrown over his head.

He fell heavily among some stones.

The horse staggered to its feet as Carita rode forward.

She knew she had to help the rider if it was at all possible for her to do so.

CHAPTER THREE

Riding *Mercury* and leading the black stallion Carita followed the farm-cart on which the two men had lifted the Stranger.

When she reached him she had found he was unconscious.

She realised that when he fell his head had struck one of the big stones that were lying outside the rim of the pit.

She had dismounted and was wondering what she should do.

Then to her relief she saw, coming round the narrow lane from which she had entered the field, a farm-cart.

She waved and shouted, and the men after opening the gate drove slowly towards her.

There was no need for explanations; they could see what had happened.

One of them patted the stallion who was still shivering from the shock of the fall.

Then the other one said:

"We'd better tak' 'e t' th' farm."

They picked up the Stranger and lifted him carefully into the cart.

Then one of them – they were both very young, no more than boys – helped her into the saddle.

He handed her the stallion's reins and she understood as he said;

"Ye follow us?"

She nodded and they set off slowly only stopping to shut the gate having passed through it.

It was about half-a-mile to the Farmhouse, which was a long, low brick building.

It was picturesque with a creeper climbing up the outside walls.

It was obviously very old.

But it was large enough for Carita to wonder if she could persuade them to let her stay there for the night.

She was feeling very tired and hungry, and she knew that *Mercury* was feeling the same.

The stallion after his fall was quite docile and moved along beside her as if he was somewhat dazed.

The boys did not drive to the front of the Farmhouse but round to the back where there was a stableyard.

Carita saw there was plenty of room for the horses.

They pulled the cart to a stand-still outside the back door.

Then one of them hurried into the house shouting:

"Ma! Ma!"

The other boy came towards Carita and said:

"Oi'll show ye t'stables."

He walked across the yard and she followed him, dismounting at the stable-door.

She was glad to see there was quite a number of stalls, some of which contained cart-horses.

In others there were riding horses, but inferior to *Mercury* and the Stranger's horse.

Two of the stalls were empty, and with the help of the boy she put the two horses into them.

By this time an elderly man had joined them and asked:

"Wot's bin a-'appenin'?"

"Accident, Jake," the boy said. "'Elp us wi' t'horses."

Jake was even less talkative than the boy was.

But he took *Mercury*'s bridle off with what Carita realised were experienced hands and started to undo his girth.

Carita saw there was fresh straw in the stall and hay in the mangers.

She patted the stallion, then as the boy walked across the yard she followed him.

She was hoping that 'Ma', whoever she might be, would be sympathetic to her plight.

She entered the Farmhouse by the back door and found it was very attractive inside.

There were heavy oak beams on the ceiling and a large open fireplace.

The boy had disappeared and she was wondering what she should do when she heard the sound of voices coming from upstairs.

She knew then that that was where they had taken the Stranger.

She thought it would be polite at least to see how he was.

She went up the oak staircase and saw an open door through which she had heard the voices.

She went in a little nervously.

A large, apple-cheeked woman was bending over the bed, and was, Carita thought, exactly how she would have expected a Farmer's wife to look.

Beside her was another older woman, wearing an apron and a mob-cap over her hair.

The latter was removing the Stranger's riding-boots while he lay stretched out on the bed with his eyes closed.

There was a wound still bleeding on his forehead against his hairline.

The two women were talking to each other, and the two boys who had brought him to the Farm were watching.

It was the Farmer's wife who saw Carita first.

"Ah, there y'are!" she exclaimed. "Me sons are a-tellin' me there's bin accident at t'pit. If Oi've told 'em once, Oi've told 'em a dozen times not t'leave it open, but there!"

She gave a sigh and went on:

"Do they ever listen t'me? An' Oi'll eat me 'at if they ever finds sight or sound o' th' spring as they've been told be there!"

"There be a spring roight enough, Ma," one of the boys said.

As he spoke he walked across the room and passing Carita went down the stairs followed by his brother.

Carita moved towards the bed and looking at the Stranger asked:

"Do you think he is badly injured?"

"No don't ye go frettin' yerself," the Farmer's wife answered. "If Oi knows anythin' about it, yer 'usband's just got slight concussion, an' 'e'll be 'isself again in a few days."

Carita parted her lips to say that he was not her husband but a strange man she had never seen until his accident.

Suddenly it struck her that this was where she could hide if her Stepfather was searching for her.

He would be asking about a young single woman, not somebody who was married and was with her husband.

It was as if this was the answer to her prayer for help.

Perhaps this explained why without really thinking about it she had put on her mother's wedding-ring.

"Do you think you will be able to get a . . Nurse for . . him?" she asked.

"A Nurse?" the Farmer's wife asked. "Now what'd ye be wantin' a Nurse for? Jessie an' me, we'll nurse 'im back t'health, won't we, Jessie?"

The other woman who had managed by now to remove both riding-boots murmured something that sounded like an affirmative.

The Farmer's wife went on:

"Seein' 'ow young ye look I'm guessin' ye baint bin married very long, but ye'll learn. When ye've got a 'usband and four sons like Oi've got, there's always one o' them in th' wars o' one sort o' another. Oi often says as Oi've bandaged more limbs than Oi've 'ad 'ot dinners!"

She laughed at her own joke and it was a very cheerful sound.

"It is very kind of you," Carita said, "and thank you very much for . . having u . . us."

She blushed as she said the last word.

But the Farmer's wife had started to undress the Stranger so did not notice.

She merely looked up to say:

"Now, Jessie'll show ye t' yer room next door where yer'll 'ave t' sleep while yer man be unconscious an' ye can unpack any baggage ye've got wi' ye."

57

Before Carita could answer Jessie had walked across the room and opened a communicating door.

The bedroom in which the stranger was lying was large with a big bow window.

The room next to it was small and narrow.

It was, Carita thought, exactly what she wanted at the moment.

She could only thank both her Guardian Angel and her Father for looking after her.

"I have my things on the back of my horse," she said to Jessie. "I will go and fetch them."

Jessie who was obviously a woman of few words grunted and started to take the cover off the bed.

Carita could see it was already made up with clean sheets and pillow-cases.

There was another door which opened onto the landing.

She went down the stairs and back into the stables.

Her saddle with the bag attached to it was hung up on a hook on the wall opposite *Mercury*'s stall.

Jake had disappeared, and now there were oats in the mangers besides the hay which both horses were munching happily.

Carita saw the buckets had also been replenished with fresh water.

Carrying her saddle-bag she walked back to the Farmhouse saying a little prayer of thankfulness.

She knew now how frightened she had been all day in case her Stepfather should catch up with her.

If he did, it would be impossible for her to escape again.

She knew he would enjoy beating her into submission.

"I hate him! I hate him!" she told herself.

She thought that if she stayed only for two days on the farm it would give *Mercury* a chance to rest before they set off again for Norfolk.

When she went upstairs again to the bedroom she found that the Farmer's wife and Jessie had undressed the Stranger and got him into bed.

He was wearing a white nightshirt which she supposed must belong to the Farmer, or to one of his sons.

Now as his face was turned towards her she could see how handsome he was.

"Oi'm just goin' t'put a bandage on yer 'usband's wound," the Farmer's wife said when she saw her. "It's not deep but 'e'll have a bruise there for th' best of a week!"

"You are sure he will regain consciousness before that?" Carita asked.

"Oi 'spects so," the Farmer's wife answered. "It just depends 'ow quick 'e 'eals 'imself. Oi lays all th' blame for this accident on me sons. They never listens to me – none of them!"

Jessie was picking up the Stranger's clothes which were stained with mud from his fall.

She emptied his pockets and put their contents on top of a chest-of-drawers.

Carita looked at them in surprise.

She could see a purse full of coins and there was a wallet which was stuffed with notes.

The Farmer's wife followed the direction of her eyes.

"Ye'd better take care o' yer 'usband's money," she said, "an' keep it safe. Oi don't want no one sayin' they left me 'ouse wi' less than when they comes into it!"

Reluctantly Carita walked towards the chest.

"Pick it up," the Farmer's wife said as if she was

speaking to a child. "There be a drawer in yer room which yer can lock."

"It is very kind of you to . . have us," Carita said, "and of course . . we must . . pay our . . way."

The Farmer's wife laughed.

"Oi'll talk 'bout that wi' yer 'usband when 'e wakes an' if he be feelin' well enough. If anythin' it's them boys as should be payin' ye! Diggin' a 'ole into which any o' our cattle or sheep mighta fallen, an' not covering it over!"

Carita wanted to say that they could hardly have expected a stallion as big as the Stranger's to come leaping over it.

She was however so thankful to know she could stay at the farm for the night that she merely picked up the Stranger's purse and wallet.

She was moving towards the door leading to her room when the Farmer's wife said.

"There now, Oi've never asked ye yer name, an' Oi doubts if ye've asked mine."

"No," Carita said, "and it would be very kind of you if you would tell me yours."

She was wondering frantically as she spoke what she could call herself.

"Johnson be me name," the Farmer's wife said, "an' there's bin Johnsons on this 'ere farm for three generations!"

"My name is Freeman," Carita answered.

It was the first name that came into her head.

She thought it somehow appropriate as she was in hiding.

"Well Mrs. Freeman," Mrs. Johnson said, "Oi' be glad we can be of service to ye, an' Oi suggests as Mr. Johnson'll be 'ome at any minute ye takes off yer ridin' 'at and comes downstairs an' 'as a bite t'eat."

"I would be very glad to do that," Carita replied, "because I am very hungry."

As she spoke she knew she was feeling weak.

It was however not only because she was hungry, but also because of the shock of everything that had happened.

"Ye hurry now," Mrs. Johnson said.

Carita went into her room and for a moment she sat down on the side of the bed.

She felt as if the world was whirling around her.

How was it possible that so much could have happened so quickly?

And yet, when she was most apprehensive about the night that lay ahead she had been saved by a Stranger.

"He is a Gentleman," she told herself reassuringly, "and I am sure he will not mind my pretending to be his wife for tonight, at any rate."

Then she told herself that, if there was any likelihood of his being disagreeable about it, she could slip away before he was well enough to continue his journey.

She took off her riding-hat.

She was about to remove her jacket when she remembered the jewellery she had sewn into it.

If Jessie, or anyone else saw the brooches, they would certainly think it strange.

Then she remembered the Stranger's money.

She found the drawer without any difficulty.

There was only one piece of furniture in the room apart from the bed and a small wardrobe.

It was a chest-of-drawers, obviously a very old one

which had probably been in the house since it was first built.

In one of the drawers there was a keyhole with a key in it.

Carita placed the Stranger's money in the drawer first.

Then, folding her riding-jacket, she found there was just enough room for her to push it into the drawer.

When she had locked it she was not certain where she should put the key for safety.

Then she remembered something she had seen her Mother do when she was a child and they were leaving the house to go for a walk.

She slipped it under a corner of the carpet.

It was unlikely that anybody would look for it there.

Having washed her hands and face in cold water she hurried down the stairs.

The Johnson family were already seated round the large table in the kitchen.

It too was a large room with a beamed ceiling from which hung two hams, a large number of onions, a duck and three unplucked hens.

Farmer Johnson was a middle-aged man growing a little stout and beginning to lose his hair.

He was standing at the end of the table carving a large leg of lamb.

Mrs. Johnson was at the other end.

There were three young men including the two boys who had picked up the Stranger, and a girl of about fourteen.

Because of the resemblance it was obvious to Carita that she was their sister.

Jessie was bringing the food to the table from the stove.

Once she had set it down there was a place for her next to Mrs. Johnson.

"Ah, there y'are, m'dear," Mrs. Johnson said as Carita appeared. "Oi be 'opin' ye wouldn' be too long or your dinner'll get cold. Oi think ye knows my two sons Billy an' Luke, their friend Jim, an' this 'ere's my daughter Molly, and me 'usband's at the end of the table."

Carita walked up to Mr. Johnson.

"How do you do," she said. "It is very kind of you and your wife to let us stay with you. I do not know what I would have done if your sons had not come along at exactly the right moment."

"'Evnin'," Farmer Johnson said.

Before he could say any more his wife exclaimed from her end of the table:

"Now sit ye down, Mrs. Freeman, an' Oi knows ye needs plenty inside yer belly after wot ye've bin through!"

Farmer Johnson put down in front of her a plate that was piled high with lamb.

There was a vast quantity of potatoes, peas and carrots to go with it.

She wondered how she would ever get through it.

By the time she had finished, Carita felt she would never feel hungry again.

The family was so busy eating that they hardly spoke a word.

Only Mrs. Johnson carried on a running conversation to which nobody appeared to pay any attention.

"Oi've jus' bin wonderin' where ye was a-goin'," she said as Carita was eating her way through the lamb.

Jessie put a cup of coffee in front of her, but she noticed that the men were all drinking cider.

She would have preferred a glass of that herself.

But she was too shy to ask for it, thinking perhaps it was entirely a male prerogative.

She was just about to answer Mrs. Johnson by saying she was going to Norfolk when she thought that might be unwise.

Perhaps, although it was unlikely, her Stepfather might recall that she had an Uncle living in Norfolk.

He was not likely to think of it.

Yet when she was writing to her relatives about her Mother's death she had mentioned to him that her Uncle had now inherited the title and was Lord Wensley of Wen.

Anyway, it would be dangerous to take chances.

Quickly, remembering that Suffolk bordered with Norfolk she answered:

"We are on our way to Essex."

"Ah, that be a long way!" Mrs. Johnson replied, "an' 'praps it be providential that ye should stop an' rest a while. Oi've always found ridin' very tirin', as me family knows."

The family bending over their plates paid no attention and Mrs. Johnson went on:

"Father tells me ye've got two fine 'orses there, an' ye needn't worry about 'em either. Jake's a dab 'and wi' 'orse-flesh, isn't he, boys?"

There was a pause before one of them, and Carita thought it was the one called Billy, answered:

"Ay, Ma, that 'e be!"

The lamb was followed by a roly-poly pudding filled with currants and with thick treacle to pour over it.

After only a few mouthfuls Carita knew she could eat no more and was wondering if it would cause offence to say so.

Then she felt sometime moving against her legs.

She realised it was a Spaniel which she had noticed when she came into the room.

There were two of them under the table.

As she surreptitiously fed them small pieces of her pudding there was no doubt it was gratefully received.

When the meal was finished the boys pushed back their chairs and walked out of the room.

"Don't forget t' lock up th' hens!" Farmer Johnson shouted after them.

There was an 'Aye', in the distance as they walked towards the back door.

When they had gone Mrs. Johnson explained to Carita:

"We 'as to shut up everythin' at night. There be foxes nosin' around to eat anythin' that moves! Farming be difficult enough wi'out they foxes havin' t'be kept so's the Gentry can hunt them, an' they only catches one out of three!"

Carita smiled.

She had learned while living at Haldon Hall that this was a constant complaint amongst the Farmers.

Sir Mortimer however had always complained there were in fact not enough foxes and if he had his way he would specially rear them.

Even to think of him made Carita shudder and she said to Mrs. Johnson;

"As I am very tired, I hope you will excuse me if I go to bed now."

"Of course, dear, ye do that," Mrs. Johnson said kindly. "Oi'll come up wi' ye now an' see if yer man's all right. If ye leave th' door open and 'e's restless in th' night, ye'll 'ear 'im right enough."

Carita wanted to ask in that case what she should do.

But she was afraid Mrs. Johnson would think that strange, so kept silent.

As if Mrs. Johnson knew what she was thinking, she said:

"Oi told Jessie to boil up some herbs that'll send 'im back to sleep if 'e wakes. Just ye give them to 'im an' 'e'll realise who ye are."

Carita knew that as he had never seen her before in his life the Stranger certainly would not recognise her.

That was something she had to keep to herself and she therefore simply said:

"I know my . . h.husband will be very grateful when he recovers."

She stumbled over the word 'husband' but Mrs. Johnson did not notice.

They reached the bedroom and there were two candles alight by the bed.

It was obvious that the Stranger had not moved since she had last seen him.

She thought once again how handsome he was.

But why, when he owned such a magnificent stallion and was obviously rich, was he riding alone without a groom?

When Mrs. Johnson said goodnight she went to her own room and started to undress.

She could not help feeling that it would be very disappointing if she left before the Stranger recovered consciousness.

Then she would never learn who he was or where he was going.

She said her prayers and said over and over again how grateful she was that she was able to spend the night in comfort and safety.

She knew if she had stayed alone at an Inn the Landlord would have thought it extraordinary.

And she would have been unable to sleep through fear that her Stepfather would arrive and find her.

In that case she would be escorted back to Haldon Hall ignominiously.

Doubtless when they got back he would beat her for running away.

'I cannot .. bear it .. I .. cannot!' she cried in terror.

Resolutely she pulled the sheets and blankets around her shoulders.

Tonight, whatever else happened, she was safe!

She must keep calm and plan what she would do next.

Then, because she was very tired, she fell asleep.

. . . .

It was morning when Carita awoke.

Her first thought was one of consternation that she had slept so heavily.

If the Stranger had called out she would not have heard him.

Quickly she got out of bed and went into the next room.

He was lying in the same position in which she had left him last night and she gave a little sigh of relief.

She could hear movements downstairs and remembered that farming people started the day very early.

She thought she would do the same.

She therefore washed in cold water and dressed herself in one of the muslin gowns she had brought with her.

She leaned out of the window and decided it was going to be a hot day.

She went downstairs to find that the men of the family had already finished their breakfast.

There was only Mrs. Johnson, Jessie and Molly in the kitchen.

"Ah, there ye are, me dear!" Mrs. Johnson exclaimed. "Oi'm sure ye're feelin' better after a good nights' sleep."

"I slept peacefully," Carita smiled.

"When Oi looks in this marnin' Oi knowed ye 'usband hadn't disturbed ye," Mrs. Johnson said. "But there – Oi knows of old concussion be like that an' they be still as a mouse 'til they get to throwin' themselves about, an' talkin' nonsense."

"And . . and what do . . I do then?" Carita asked.

Mrs. Johnson smiled at her.

"Now don't ye go worryin' yer 'ead about yer man. Oi'll look after 'e, as Oi've looked after Father, an' that there Billy, 'e's always in trouble of one sort of 'nother. Th' times Oi've bandaged 'e, Oi couldn't tell ye."

Carita smiled.

If Mrs. Johnson was going to look after the Stranger, then she need not worry about him.

She ate a large plate of eggs and bacon which Jessie gave her.

Then she went out to look at the horses.

They were obviously rested.

At the same time she thought the stallion was a little listless, but was reassured by Jake.

"E'll be orl right tomorrer," Jake said, "an' a finer 'orse Oi've never seen."

The way he spoke made Carita feel jealous for *Mercury*.

68

She went into his stall to make a fuss of him.

"There is no one more beautiful than you!" she told him.

As he nuzzled against her she thought he was in fact the only friend she had in the whole world and she could never lose him.

"I am sure we will be all right when we reach Norfolk," she told herself reassuringly.

At the same time she felt afraid in case her Uncle would not let her stay with him.

Her Father had always said what a very strange man he was.

"He ought to have been a monk, or like the *fakirs* in India who sit on top of a mountain meditating on the Life that comes after this one," she had once heard her Father say.

"Why do they do that, Papa?" Carita had asked.

"Heaven knows!" her Father had answered. "I have quite enough to do concerning myself with this life without bothering about the next!"

Yet, however light-hearted he had been then, she was sure that wherever he was now, he was thinking about her and helping her.

"I need your help, Papa," she said in her heart. "I need it desperately. You know I cannot marry Lord Stilbury, but if Step-papa finds me I will have to give in rather than have him beat me."

She felt herself shudder once again as she thought of it.

Then she put her arms round *Mercury*.

She clung to him as if he was all that was left who could protect her from the horror and degradation that her Stepfather had planned for her.

When she went back into the house she asked

Mrs. Johnson if there was anything she could do for her.

Mrs. Johnson considered for a moment. Then she said:

"Are ye handy with a needle?"

"Yes, of course," Carita answered.

"Then ye could 'elp me by doin' some darnin'," Mrs. Johnson said. "Them boys wears out their socks quicker than Oi can mend them."

"Of course I will do that for you," Carita said.

Mrs. Johnson produced a pile of socks and stockings which had been washed.

However they all had holes either in the toes or the heels.

There was the wool with which to mend them and Carita carried them upstairs to the Stranger's bedroom in a basket.

It grew hotter as the day wore on.

She sat in the window sewing and occasionally glanced towards the bed.

It was very peaceful with just the hum of the bees outside the window and the distant sounds of the hens.

There was too the song of the birds as they flew over the overgrown garden out into the fields beyond.

Carita kept stopping her work to look out.

She thought that she might have stepped into another world from the one she had just left.

Then unexpectedly there was a sound from the bed.

She put down the stocking she was holding in her hand and rose to her feet.

The Stranger was turning over onto his side and moving his head from side to side.

She reached him and realised that his eyes were still closed.

His lips were open and she thought perhaps his mouth was dry.

She had noticed when she came in that the herbs which Jessie had brewed were in a jug beside the bed.

She poured out half a glass.

Slipping her arm behind his head she raised the Stranger from the pillow.

He moved his hand and she was half afraid he would knock over the glass and make a mess.

Then she said quietly:

"You are thirsty. You must drink. It will do you good and you will go to sleep again."

As she spoke she seemed to remember her mother talking to her when as a child she had been ill.

She was sure it was the right thing to do.

Perhaps even though he was unconscious he would be vaguely aware of what was happening.

He certainly drank down most of what she had poured into the glass.

Then as she lowered his head back onto the pillow she thought he seemed rather hot.

Going to the washhand-stand she looked for a sponge and realised he had brought nothing with him.

She ran to her own room to find her sponge and a towel and brought it back.

Gently she sponged his face, then wiped it with the towel.

It was the first time she had ever done such a thing to a man.

She felt as if he was like a small boy who had fallen and hurt himself.

He needed care and to be looked after.

It was either her ministrations or the herbs, but he was quiet.

He did not move when she went down for a mid-day meal.

Later in the afternoon Mrs. Johnson came up to see how he was.

"Do you think he has a fever?" Carita asked.

"Tomorrow," Mrs. Johnson said, "we'll wash 'im. When there's a fever that usually brings it down, an' Oi must say it's 'ot today as Oi've ever knowed it!"

Carita knew she would find it very embarrassing to wash the Stranger, but she could hardly refuse to help.

"Perhaps he will be conscious tomorrow," she replied, "then he can wash himself."

Mrs. Johnson shook her head.

"The longer 'e sleeps the better," she said, "and don't yer go disturbing 'e afore ye 'as to."

She smiled as she spoke and put a hand on Carita's arm.

"'E be a fine upstandin' man," she said, "an' Oi understands ye wants 'is arms round ye, but there – ye'll just 'ave to be patient."

Carita felt shy, but there was nothing she could say.

"Now come along downstairs," Mrs. Johnson said. "I can see ye've darned them socks for me, so we'll cook somethin' really good for dinner."

"I would like to help you with that," Carita said.

"'Course ye can," Mrs. Johnson smiled, "and don't forget, when 'e wakes ye'll 'ave to fatten 'e up. He'll need it and it'll stop him feelin' angry at havin' a fall. There's never been a man yet as wants to admit 'twas 'is own fault!"

She laughed as she spoke and Carita followed her down the stairs.

She thought that perhaps one day all this advice

would come in useful when she really had a husband.

Then at the mere idea she was frightened.

Once again she was praying:

"But not Lord Stilbury . . please, God . . not Lord Stilbury! Any man . . but not . . him!"

. . . .

The dinner they had that night Carita thought was delicious.

She had helped Mrs. Johnson prepare several young chickens.

After that, instead of a heavy roly-poly pudding, they made a jelly and a fruit salad with fruit they collected from the garden.

There was thick cream to go with it.

Carita thought it was a meal her mother would have enjoyed if they had only been able to afford it.

When she went upstairs again she was singing a little song to herself.

The Stranger was still asleep and Mrs. Johnson had put a fresh jug of herbs beside his bed.

Carita undressed.

Because it was still so hot she only covered herself with a sheet.

She must have been asleep for about an hour when she heard a sound from next door.

She had pulled back the curtains before she got into bed.

Now the moonlight was streaming in through her window.

It enabled her to get out of bed quickly and run through the open door to where the Stranger lay.

On Mrs. Johnson's advice she had left two lighted candles beside his bed.

If he should call out she would be able to make her way to him without having to search for a light.

One glance at the bed told Carita that the Stranger was very restless.

At the same time, he was trying to say something.

Quickly she poured out the herbs.

Then kneeling beside the bed she put her arm behind his head as she had done before.

"What you need is a drink," she said, "then you will go back to sleep again."

She was raising the glass to his lips when she saw that his eyes were open.

They were grey eyes, and she was aware he was staring at her.

She was, however, not quite certain whether he could see her or not.

"Just drink," she said, "and you will feel better."

She moved the glass nearer.

Then in a deep voice which seemed to come from a long distance the Stranger asked:

"W.who – are you – and – where – am I?"

CHAPTER FOUR

Carita awoke to the sound of voices in the next room.

She knew it was Mrs. Johnson and thought she must be talking to the Stranger.

It occurred to Carita that if she referred to his wife and he had no idea who or what she meant, it could be very uncomfortable.

She got out of bed and began to dress quickly.

She could hear Mrs. Johnson talking without a pause, and occasionally laughing.

As she moved towards the communicating-door she heard her say;

"Oi'll go downstairs an' get ye some breakfast an' yer'll feel better with somethin' inside ye."

Carita waited until she heard the footsteps on the stairs.

Then she went into the bedroom.

The Stranger was sitting up propped against his pillows.

He looked at her quizzically as she came in.

Because she was frightened she went nearer to him and said in a whisper:

"I will explain . . everything . . but they think . . we

are married and please . . do not . . tell them we . . are not."

The words seemed to tumble over themselves as she spoke.

"Married?" the Stranger repeated slowly.

"Yes . . but please . . please wait . . until we are alone . . and I will . . explain."

He was staring at her with what she thought was an incredulous look in his eyes.

Before he could speak, however, Jessie came into the room carrying a tray.

She walked up to the bed and put it down beside him, then whisked the cover off the plate.

On it Carita could see eggs and bacon, which she was sure would also be waiting for her downstairs in the kitchen.

Without saying anything she hurried down the stairs.

It was better, she thought, to let the Stranger eat before she went into explanations.

"Perhaps he will be . . very angry," she murmured. "In which case, the . . sooner I can get . . away the . . better!"

Because she was worried she ate what was put in front of her without speaking.

There was no need to speak anyway, as Mrs. Johnson had a lot to say.

"Oi didn't think a strong man like yer 'usband would be long in a-comin' round an' although Oi'm not sayin' Jessie's herbs didn't help 'im, when it comes down to 'brass tacks' it's yer own strength that counts."

As Carita was contemplating this the two boys got up from the table and left.

The Farmer had already gone before she had come downstairs.

Mrs. Johnson finished by saying that Carita's 'husband' must not do too much.

"'Never run afore yer can walk', that's wot Oi says after many years experience. There be no hurry for ye to leave us. We likes 'avin' yer 'ere, and that's th' truth."

"You have been very kind," Carita murmured, "and thank you for a lovely breakfast!"

She should have gone upstairs again.

Instead, feeling shy, she went out to the stables, to see if *Mercury* was all right.

He was moving restlessly in his stall, as was the stallion.

She knew that what they needed was exercise.

"We may have to leave today," she whispered to *Mercury*.

She felt her heart sink at the idea of going off 'into the blue' and finding her way alone to Norfolk.

Having told herself she must not be a coward she went upstairs.

As she reached the bedroom, Jessie came out carrying a tray on which there was a small jug of hot water and a used razor.

The Stranger had shaved himself.

When Carita saw him she thought that it made him even more handsome than he had been yesterday when he was unconscious.

She shut the door behind her and moved slowly towards the bed.

Because she was frightened her eyes seemed to fill her face.

When she reached the bed she found it impossible to speak.

The Stranger looked at her and unexpectedly he smiled.

"Now what is all this about?" he asked. "Suppose you sit down and tell me?"

Jessie had removed his bandage.

Although there was a large bruise on his forehead, the wound was partially healed and was covered by a scab.

Because her legs felt weak Carita sat down thankfully on the chair which was beside the bed.

"I . . I saw you . . f.fall," she began hesitatingly.

"What was on the other side of that hedge?" the Stranger asked. "I realised as I went over it that I was a fool not to have made sure that *Jupiter* could land safely."

"'Jupiter'? So that is his name! He is the most magnificent stallion I have ever seen!"

"Thank you, I am glad you admire him."

"Of course I admire him, and strangely enough my horse is called *Mercury*!"

The Stranger smiled.

"Then we are definitely invoking the same gods, and I suppose that as I have heard that *Jupiter* is unhurt I should be grateful."

"Your head struck a large stone," Carita said.

"What were stones doing in a country field?" he asked in surprise.

"I understand the men have been digging to find an underground spring which they think is there below the hedge."

There was silence before the Stranger said:

"I have no one to blame but myself, and the sooner I am on my way the better!"

Carita gave a little cry.

"You must not move too quickly! You had concussion! You have been unconscious for forty-eight hours and your head is still damaged."

78

The Stranger put his hand up to his wound and touched it lightly as if he was aware it would hurt him to do so.

Then he said:

"These Farm people have been very kind in having us here, but tell me why you had to say we were married."

Carita looked away and he saw the colour come into her cheeks.

He thought it was like the dawn breaking in the sky and that she was surprisingly beautiful.

At the same time he had no wish to become involved with any young woman, but only to escape from Imogen.

Everything that had happened had come back to his mind when he woke.

He had lain thinking of it until Mrs. Johnson had looked into the room to see if he was awake.

It was then she had drawn back the curtains and started to talk.

Carita in a small voice, which told him how nervous she was, replied to his question:

"I . . I was . . running away . . and because I was . . alone . . I had no idea . . where I could . . stay the night."

The Stranger did not speak and she went on:

"When your stallion fell and . . threw you and . . you hit your head against a stone I . . wondered what I . . should do."

"And what did you do?" he asked.

"Fortunately I saw a farm-cart coming down the lane with two young men in it and they . . came when I . . hailed them."

"So they put me into the cart and brought me back to the farm!" the Stranger finished.

Carita nodded.

"Before I could . . say anything Mrs. Johnson assumed that we were . . married . . and I knew that meant I had . . somewhere to . . stay for . . the night."

The Stranger smiled.

"So it was as easy as that!"

"Y.yes . . and I also . . thought," Carita went on, "that if . . anyone was . . looking for . . me they would not . . expect me to have a . . husband."

"I believe Mrs. Johnson addressed me as 'Mr. Freeman'," the Stranger said. "Is that the name you chose for me?"

"It was . . the first name that . . came into my head."

"It is not your own?"

"No."

"And are you going to tell me your real name?"

There was silence and again she looked away from him before she said:

"I think it would be . . better if it remains a secret . . I am so afraid . . so desperately . . afraid that . . those who will be looking for me . . might somehow become aware that . . I am here."

She gave a little shiver as she spoke.

There was silence until the Stranger said:

"I can see you are frightened, but surely you should not be travelling alone. Would you like to tell me where you are going?"

Carita hesitated before she said:

"I am going to . . try and reach my . . Uncle who lives in . . Norfolk . . but I told Mrs. Johnson that . . we were on our way to Essex . . just in case she was . . questioned."

"I imagine that is unlikely," the Stranger said quietly. "You appear to me to have covered your tracks very cleverly."

"I am praying so . . at the same time . . I still have a long way to go . . and even then I . . may not be . . safe."

She was thinking that her Uncle might be unwilling to have her with him and would turn her away.

Alternatively her Stepfather might trace her there.

He might persuade her Uncle into thinking it was sensible for her to marry a rich and important man.

She had no idea that the fear in her eyes and the tension in her body was very obvious to the Stranger.

After a moment he said in a very much more gentle voice than he had used before:

"Can you not trust me with your secret? Perhaps I can find a solution to your problem."

"No one can do that . . unless they can hide . . me from my . . Stepfather," Carita said frantically.

"So it is a Stepfather from whom you are running away!" the Stranger said.

Carita thought she had been indiscreet.

At the same time she could not retract what she had said, so she merely nodded.

"Is your Mother dead?" the Stranger enquired.

"Yes, and that is why . . my Stepfather is now my . . Guardian."

There was silence. Then the Stranger said:

"I am making a guess – and I may be wrong – but I think your Stepfather is trying to make you marry somebody you dislike."

Carita stared at him.

"H.how can you possibly . . know that?"

"I told you – I am rather good at solving problems," the Stranger replied.

He settled himself a little more comfortably against his pillows before he went on:

"I think, as you have bound us together in what is a very intimate position as man and wife, you should let me try to help you. It is the least I can do after you have rescued me."

"I expect . . if I had ridden on . . you would have been . . found . . eventually," Carita said.

"You cannot be sure of that. A night in the open might have proved very bad for me, and somebody might have stolen *Jupiter*!"

Carita gave a little cry.

"That would have been . . terrible! I know how I would feel if . . somebody stole *Mercury* from . . me."

"It is certainly a possibility if you ride alone."

Carita stared at him.

"I never thought of . . that! Now you are making me more frightened than I am . . already!"

"Instead of being frightened, suppose you 'put your cards on the table', and start by telling me your Christian name, which is certainly something Mrs. Johnson will expect me to know."

"It is . . Carita."

"Is that true?"

"Yes, it is."

"It is a very attractive name," the Stranger remarked, "and mine is Darol."

"That is unusual."

"You have not heard it before?"

"I do not think so."

"Now let me suggest that we start at the beginning

82

and you tell me why you do not wish to marry the man your Stepfather has chosen for you."

Carita drew in her breath.

"He is . . horrible . . very old . . and cruel! They say his first wife . . died because he . . beat her . . to death! He is also . . cruel to . . his horses."

She spoke in a quiet voice so that the Earl could hardly hear her.

Yet he knew that every word she uttered was sincere and truthful.

He felt he would have known if she had lied to him.

He was also aware that no woman, however clever, could have faked the little shudder that went through her whole body.

Nor the terror which darkened her eyes.

When she had finished speaking he asked:

"Why does your Stepfather wish you to marry anyone who is so unpleasant?"

"Because he is . . very rich and . . important, and it would be of social . . benefit to my Stepfather to be able to speak of him as his . . son-in-law."

As Carita spoke she was remembering the elation there had been in her Stepfather's voice as he had said that Lord Stilbury would be, 'to all intents and purposes, my son-in-law.'

"So you ran away! I think it was very sensible of you!" the Earl approved.

"You understand . . you really understand! How could I . . marry a man like that . . and Step-papa said that if I would not agree he would . . beat me until . . I did!"

Now there was no mistaking the horror in Carita's voice.

"Do you really think he meant it?" the Earl asked in astonishment. "Has he ever beaten you before?"

"Once . . when I was . . sixteen," Carita answered, "and it was . . horrible . . degrading . . but he . . enjoyed doing it . . I know he . . enjoyed it . . and he wants to . . do it again!"

She felt the tears come into her eyes and her whole body was shaking.

She jumped up from the chair and went to the window.

She stood there looking out, fighting for self-control.

She had not realised it would hurt her so much to speak of it.

Yet now she was telling somebody for the first time what she had turned over in her thoughts.

It seemed even more appalling and evil than it had before.

Lying back against his pillows the Earl saw the sunshine on her hair and the slimness of her body in the thin muslin gown.

He found it hard to believe that any man, however debauched, could whip anything so delicate and so fragile.

A few minutes elapsed before he said:

"Come back, Carita, and let us plan how I can help you to escape."

She turned round and it was for the moment as if the sunshine filled her eyes.

"Do . . you mean . . that?" she asked. "Do you . . really mean . . it?"

"Of course I mean it," the Earl replied, "but we will have to be very clever about it."

She ran back to the bed and instead of sitting on the chair she knelt down.

It was as she had done when she had given him the herbal drink and washed his face.

"If you will . . help me," she said, "perhaps I have a chance of getting . . away."

"Of course you have to get away," the Earl said firmly. "First, as you have already said, it is unlikely that your Stepfather will be looking for you with a husband."

"You do . . really . . understand!" Carita said. "It is very . . very . . wonderful of . . you!"

The Earl was used to women telling him how wonderful he was, but he thought he had never before heard it said with such sincerity.

"What we must not do," he said, "is to make any mistakes. Now tell me how far you travelled yesterday."

"I . . I do not know . . exactly," Carita said. "I left at dawn when I knew there would be . . no one awake. When I went to the stables the only groom on duty was asleep, and did not . . hear me . . go."

The Earl smiled to himself.

He had left at the same time and he had reckoned he had less than twenty miles to cover before he reached home.

But it was a very different story to get this child, for she was little more, to Norfolk.

He was thinking that perhaps the best thing he could do would be to find somewhere for her to stay in his village.

He could not arrive at The Priory accompanied by a beautiful young woman without causing a great deal of gossip.

"If I find her somewhere to stay," he thought, "I will then get in touch with her relative in Norfolk so that he can come and fetch her rather than her going alone to him."

85

Aloud he said:

"Tell me about your Uncle. Do you think he will be able to prevent your Stepfather from forcing you into a marriage which terrifies you? Could he give you the opportunity of meeting a man you would like to marry?"

"The fact . . is," Carita said in a low voice, "I have not . . seen Uncle Andrew for a . . very long time. Papa always said he was a . . strange man and . . ought to have been a . . Monk. He has . . cut himself off from . . the world and prefers being a . . recluse."

The Earl was startled.

"I have heard there are people like that," he said, "although I have never met one."

"He may . . refuse to . . have me," Carita said. "Then I shall have to find . . somewhere else to go . . or perhaps find employment of . . some kind."

"You have no money?" the Earl enquired.

"None of my own," Carita admitted, "but I have brought with me my mother's jewellery."

She paused for a moment before she said:

"I . . I was going to . . ask you if you would . . be kind enough to . . pay what . . I owe when we . . leave here . . then when I have sold one of my mother's brooches . . I could . . pay . . you back."

"That reminds me," the Earl remarked. "What happened to the money I had with me?"

"I have locked it in a drawer in my room which Mrs. Johnson suggested I should do," Carita explained quickly.

"Then you need not worry about what we owe Mrs. Johnson," the Earl said. "At the same time, your jewellery, however valuable it may be, will not last for ever."

86

"I know that," Carita said, "but I am sure I can find something to do . . perhaps teaching children . . I have been well-educated!"

The Earl did not comment on that.

He thought she was far too young to be either a School-Teacher or a Governess.

Both professions were, he knew, badly paid.

He also thought that no Lady in her senses would take into her house anyone as lovely as the girl kneeling beside him.

"I can see you are . . thinking it will be . . difficult for me to . . find work," Carita said, "but if I am . . careful I am sure Mama's jewellery will . . last for a long time . . perhaps for two years . . and then I shall be . . older."

"I do not think two years will make much difference," the Earl said. "In the meantime, Carita, as you well know, you should be chaperoned or have somebody who would really take care of you."

"I have thought and thought, and there is . . really only Uncle Andrew," Carita said. "But as he is a . . recluse he may not . . want me."

"I do see it is a problem," the Earl said, "but I cannot believe it is one to which we cannot find a solution. In the meantime you are safe here, and when we leave I will find somewhere for you to stay before you attempt the next part of your journey to Norfolk."

"Thank you . . oh . . thank you for being . . so kind!" Carita said. "I was . . afraid to go to an Inn . . I knew they would think it strange that I was alone . . and I was petrified in case my Stepfather would . . make enquiries after I had . . gone and then . . follow and catch up with me."

The fear was back in her voice and he knew she was trembling.

"Now what we have to do," he said in a calm unhurried manner, "is to relax and enjoy ourselves until we actually have to leave here. I agree with Mrs. Johnson – it would be a mistake for me to go today. I shall have to see how I feel tomorrow when I wake up."

"Please . . do not let it be . . too soon," Carita pleaded. "I am not . . only thinking of you . . but of me!"

"That is frank, at any rate!" the Earl replied. "And have you seen *Jupiter* this morning?"

"Yes, I went to see both *Jupiter* and *Mercury* before I came up to you," Carita answered. "They were both fidgeting a little and I felt they needed exercise."

"*Jupiter* will certainly not like being cooped up all the time in a stable!" the Earl remarked. "Have you asked the Farmer if he has a paddock in which the horse could move about safely."

Carita got to her feet.

"I will see to it at once!" she said.

She had been frightened for the moment that he would suggest she rode the horses.

She was afraid of doing so in case someone should see her.

Now she ran downstairs to tell Mrs. Johnson what Darol had suggested.

"Oi knowed as 'e'd be thinkin' of 'is horse first!" Mrs. Johnson said. "Oi knows men, an' it's their animals as are uppermost in their minds with us women as a poor second."

She laughed before Carita could say anything, then told her where to find Farmer Johnson.

The horses were let loose in a field from which it would be difficult for them to escape.

They ran round and round stretching their legs and bucking to show how pleased they were to be free.

Carita watched them for some time.

Then she went back into the house to tell Darol what she had arranged.

She came into the bedroom with her cheeks flushed, her hair a little untidy from the wind.

The Earl thought she might be Persephone coming back from Hades to bring Spring to the world.

"*Mercury* and *Jupiter* are having a wonderful time!" she smiled. "They asked me to thank you very much for thinking of them."

The Earl laughed and she sat down on the chair by his bed.

He deliberately refrained from talking any more about her troubles, knowing how much it upset her.

Instead they started to talk on a number of subjects.

He found she was surprisingly knowledgeable, considering how young she was.

He could not help thinking that when he was with Imogen, unless he was making love to her, the conversation was usually banal or consisted of gossip.

Invariably it became personal.

Like all the other women he had ever known, Imogen's only real interest was love and how it concerned her.

Carita told him that her Father had been a Naval Officer but without revealing his name.

She described in graphic detail the work he had been doing in Portsmouth.

Also the places he had visited when he had been at sea.

"So he died when he was in the West Indies!" the Earl remarked.

"He wrote telling Mama and me about the place, and we found books that described the island where his ship was in harbour and the other islands which sounded fascinating."

"It is somewhere I would like to go myself one day," the Earl said.

It was then Carita began to speak to him of Haiti and the Voodoo that was practised there.

She also talked of the strange things that could happen on the other islands.

"You know that the Empress Josephine was born on the island of Martinique?" she said. "A Gypsy foretold when she was quite young all the things that would happen to her."

"So you believe in Gypsy fortune-tellers!" the Earl asked.

"I think they are very picturesque, but I have no wish to have my fortune told."

"Why not?"

He thought as he asked the question it was perhaps an indiscreet one.

"I want to think that my future is going to be a beautiful and very exciting one, and of course, I hope that like Mama, I will fall in love with somebody who loves me, and we will be happy ever afterwards."

There was a rapt little note in Carita's voice which the Earl did not miss.

"Suppose the man with whom you fall in love is of no importance and has no money?" the Earl suggested.

"Why should that matter, as long as we were together?" Carita asked.

She thought the Earl looked sceptical and she said:

"Mama and Papa had very little money when they first married, and yet they were so happy that every house in which they lived seemed to be filled with love."

She gave a sigh before she said:

"That is what I knew when I was a child, and it was only when I went to live with my Stepfather that I realised that a grand house, servants and beautiful clothes were nothing but sawdust unless one had love."

The Earl's lips twisted a little.

He was thinking, as he had thought before, that many women, like Imogen had expressed their love and admiration for him.

But they would certainly not have been so voluble if he had had no title and no money.

"Do you really believe," he said aloud, "that if you fell in love now, let us say with one of the Farmer's sons, you would be prepared to marry him and work hard as Mrs. Johnson does to keep things going?"

"Of course I would!" Carita declared. "As Mama said once, when one has love one holds the moon and the stars in one's arms and nothing else is of any importance."

"Then all I can say," the Earl remarked, "is that you are a very unusual young woman."

Carita blushed.

"I think you are laughing at me!" she murmured.

After a moment she added:

"When Mama married my Stepfather, I am sure now she was thinking more of me than of herself. We were very poor and often hungry, and she worried about me."

Then in an even lower tone she went on:

"When Mama . . died she was . . united with Papa again . . and I knew how much she had . . missed him . .

91

however rich and comfortable she had been with . . my Stepfather."

There was a touch of fear in Carita's voice and the Earl said quickly:

"Well, we can only hope, Carita, that it will happen to both of us and, if you are running away, so am I. So we have that in common, and we must both take great care that we are not caught."

"*You* are . . running . . away?" Carita asked in astonishment. "But . . from whom? Who would possibly be menacing . . you?"

He did not reply, and she said after a moment:

"I . . I think perhaps it . . is a . . woman."

"Now you are trying to be perceptive," the Earl said, "and that is a mistake. You have your secrets and I have mine. At the same time, we both have to be very careful that no one catches us."

He was thinking as he spoke that if Carita's Stepfather was looking for her, Imogen would certainly be looking for him.

He was quite certain she would not give up the chase.

If it was humanly possible she would somehow get him into a situation where he would find it very hard to refuse to marry her.

It struck him that he had intended to be back at The Priory long before now.

He would have had time to tell the servants that under no circumstances were they to admit Lady Imogen Basset.

That in itself would create gossip.

Yet he could think of no other way by which he could keep her from him.

He thought that as soon as she learnt of his escape, she would go straight to London.

When she failed to find him there, she would soon appear at The Priory.

The difficulties ahead swept over him like a tidal wave.

"What am I to do? What am I do do?" he asked himself.

He knew that she would claim that he had deserted her, which would evoke a certain amount of sympathy in those she called her friends.

But his family and all the more respectable members of the *Beau Monde* would merely think he was being sensible.

"How could I ever have imagined she would go so far as to try to force me into marriage," he asked, "and have all those people present to witness the ceremony?"

They were her friends, not his, she had invited to her house-party; they were the 'Rag, Tag and Bobtail' of the Social World.

At the same time, they would talk.

The Earl felt himself squirm at the idea of his name being dragged through the dirt.

He thought of the laughter it would arouse in those who sat drinking in the Clubs of St. James's.

'The best thing I can do is to go abroad,' he thought.

Then he decided that would make things even worse than they were already.

Nobody disappeared abroad unless they were guilty of something.

He had no wish for people to say he was running away from a mess he had himself created.

Because he was very proud and fastidious he was afraid that every step he took could be more disastrous than the last.

He had been silent for so long that Carita said:

"When I was worried, as I can see you are now, I found the best thing I could do was to pray."

"Pray?" the Earl asked in surprise.

"I prayed when Step-papa first told me that I had to marry that awful man. Then God, or perhaps it was Papa, told me I had to run away. It was a difficult thing to do, but once it was in my mind it seemed to be planned out for me."

She was suddenly aware that the Earl was looking at her with a somewhat cynical expression on his face.

"What I am saying may seem . . strange," she said, "but when I was praying again that I would find somewhere to stay for the night, you had your accident, and when I came here with you I was able to stay because they thought we were married."

She paused for a moment and then smiled and continued:

"It was then I knew it had all been planned and that someone was looking after me and helping me, and I was stupid to have been so frightened."

The Earl was watching her.

He knew she was telling him this simply because she thought it would help him too.

"Thank you for telling me, Carita," he said after a moment. "Now I think of it, it is a long time since I said the prayers my mother taught me. Perhaps that is why some things in my life have gone wrong."

"If you pray I am sure they will come right," Carita said, "but never quite in the way you expect."

She gave a childlike little laugh before she added:

"Who would have guessed that you and *Jupiter* would be the answer to my prayers? Perhaps, although you may not think it now, I will be able to help you because you have helped me."

94

"I can only hope so," the Earl said. "So while you are praying for yourself, Carita, you might also pray for me."

"Of course I will!" Carita said quite unaffectedly. "I have in fact already said many prayers of gratitude that I am 'Mrs. Freeman'!"

She laughed as she spoke and the Earl laughed too.

It struck him that this was an extraordinary conversation to be having with anyone so young as Carita.

Or in fact any woman who was not as old as his Mother.

He was remembering now how his Mother had taught him to say his prayers when he was a little boy.

When he went to Eton he had thought that Chapel twice a day was a bore.

And when he was grown up there was no need to pray because everything he wanted seemed to fall into his hands like a ripe peach.

It was only now that Imogen had, and he admitted it was his own fault, forced him into an uncomfortable position from which he had had to escape.

The more he thought about it, the more he realised how foolish he had been not to realise sooner that she was determined to marry him.

Unlike the other women he had known she would not let him just vanish out of her life.

He thought of the expensive presents he had given the Beauties with whom he had had *affaires de coeur*.

While there had been tears and recriminations, there had been no scandal following their association.

And certainly not a lot of people were aware that he was a reluctant Bridegroom.

He could imagine all too well what had been said

at The Towers, and the way Imogen had raged at his disappearance.

She would also be absolutely determined to get him back.

Next time there would be no escape.

Once again the Earl was asking himself beneath his breath what the devil he could do.

Then because Carita was sitting there looking, he thought, like a small angel, he told himself it was a mistake to evoke the devil.

If she was right, it was God who would help him now.

He wondered if his was not too unimportant a problem.

Then he remembered how his Mother had said that God hears every little prayer and that his Guardian Angel was watching over him.

"I cannot think of a moment when I have needed my Guardian Angel more!" he thought.

Impulsively he put out his hand towards Carita.

"I have been thinking over what you have said to me," he told her, "and I have a feeling that with your prayers and the help of my Guardian Angel, if I have one, we both will be able to save ourselves and definitely prevent anybody from catching up with us."

Carita smiled and put out her hand to his.

His fingers closed over it and she felt how strong he was.

"I am sure you are right," she said, "and please . . let me stay with you a little while longer . . just in case the Devil is after us too!"

It flashed through the Earl's mind that that was an apt description of Imogen.

He said aloud:

"In the Story-Books Good triumphs over Evil, and the White Knight always kills the Dragon. That, Carita, is what we must do, but in my case there are two Dragons!"

CHAPTER FIVE

Carita and the Earl rode away from the farm early in the morning.

He was determined to reach The Priory as quickly as possible and find out what had happened after he ran away from The Towers.

He did not of course mention this to Carita.

All he said was that he would find her somewhere to stay when he reached the village in which he lived.

Mrs. Johnson sent them off very volubly, saying how much she had enjoyed having them at the Farm.

She gave them a large package which contained their luncheon.

"Don't ye go wastin' yer money on them Inns," she said. "They give ye tough meat an' stale cheese. Ye'll like wot Oi've packed for ye."

"I am sure we shall," Carita replied, "and thank you very, very much, Mrs. Johnson, for all your kindness."

Mrs. Johnson kissed her affectionately.

"Now ye look after yerself," she said, "or rather, tell yer 'usband to keep 'is eye on ye."

She looked at the Earl as she spoke who said:

"I promise I will do that."

Then they were off.

The Earl had insisted on paying Mrs. Johnson.

Carita knew she was overcome when she glanced at the banknote he pressed in her hand.

She had an idea it was for ten pounds.

Yet she could hardly believe anyone would give so much.

The horses were fresh and they galloped for some way to drive the mischief out of them.

After that they settled down to a steady but brisk pace.

The Earl knew it would bring them to The Priory about the middle of the afternoon.

When it was noon they were both hungry because they had had breakfast much earlier than usual.

The Earl found a delightful place on a hill just above a small valley.

It was where a wood ended and where there was a grassy patch where they could sit in the shade.

They knotted the horses' reins and let them loose.

"I do not know about *Mercury*," the Earl said, "but *Jupiter* will come when I whistle."

"You are insulting *Mercury*!" Carita replied. "He has come when I called him ever since I first rode him, and I am certain he understands every word I say."

The Earl laughed.

They sat down on the grass under the branches of an elm.

Carita opened the luncheon which Mrs. Johnson had given them.

She had certainly been very generous.

There were slices of ham and chicken, and a brawn which Carita knew was a particular delicacy of hers.

There was a sauce in a small covered cup to go with it.

Also a salad of lettuces and tomatoes from the garden.

The Earl produced a bottle of cider from his saddle-bag and two mugs from which to drink it.

Carita laughed when she saw them.

"I thought you looked as if you were leaving with more than when you arrived!" she said. "I did not realise that you were carrying anything so delicious as Farmer Johnson's cider!"

"It was heavy enough to be a handicap to *Jupiter*," he replied, "but that enabled *Mercury* to keep up with him."

He was teasing her and Carita said:

"Now you are being unkind about *Mercury* again. I think he is the most beautiful horse I have ever seen!"

"And of course I admire *Jupiter*," the Earl said. "One day we will race them and see who is the winner."

Carita did not answer.

She was thinking that there might not ever be another time in the future when she would be with Darol.

As soon as she arrived at the village where he had promised to find her somewhere to stay the night, she would have to move on again.

She could not be an encumbrance on him.

She must find her Uncle and hope that he would be kind enough to let her stay with him.

She also had the uncomfortable feeling that Darol's village, wherever that might be, was too near to her Stepfather.

She was sure he would never give up the search for her.

For now she suspected he was making plausible excuses to Lord Stilbury for her absence.

She did not, however, say anything aloud.

She thought it would seem ungrateful when Darol had been so kind in pretending to be her husband.

Besides that he had promised to help her in the future.

"He is young and he is handsome," she told herself. "I am sure he has a great number of people whom he cares for, and has no wish to add me to the list."

The Earl was eating his luncheon with relish.

"Mrs. Johnson was right," he remarked. "We should not have been able to find anything to eat as good as this at any Inn we have passed so far."

"There have not been many," Carita reminded him.

"That is because we were keeping to the fields, but there will be more villages on the next part of the journey."

He was, however, determined to avoid them, knowing that in most of them they would recognise him.

He had been wondering whether or not he should tell Carita who he was, but decided against it.

What he liked about her was her unselfconsciousness.

She had ceased to be shy or embarrassed by him.

She talked to him with a natural ease which he had never found with other women.

The women he met in London were of course the sophisticated Beauties who pursued him so ardently.

They flattered him with every word they spoke and every flutter of their eye-lashes.

He was all too familiar with their repertoire which varied little from one woman to another.

Once she had got over her first embarrassment of explaining that she had been pretending to be his wife, Carita talked to him as if he was her brother.

They had discussed, he thought, every subject under the sun without her being personal about any of them.

It was for him a new experience.

He could not help wondering why she was so different.

He could hardly believe that he did not attract her.

He knew, when he understood why she was frightened, that she had looked at him with her large eyes as if there was something god-like about him.

"She is certainly unique and very different from any other girl I have ever met!" he thought.

Then he knew that if he was truthful he had met very few.

He had deliberately avoided talking to debutantes.

He knew that even to dine with one could trap him into matrimony.

Now after his experience with Imogen he vowed he would never again have anything to do with widows.

Carita broke in on his thoughts by saying:

"That was the most delicious luncheon, but I cannot eat any more, and it seems a wicked waste to throw it away."

"It is what I am going to do with what is left of the salad," the Earl said, "and the cups."

Carita gave a little cry.

"That is extravagant! Perhaps if you put them safely under a tree somebody will find them and take them home because they will be useful."

The Earl smiled and rose to his feet to do what she had suggested.

Carita rose too and at that moment two men came through the trees on horseback.

The Earl glanced at them, then stiffened.

Both men had black handkerchiefs covering the lower parts of their faces, leaving only their eyes uncovered.

Each carried a pistol in his hand.

Too late the Earl realised that he should have brought one with him on such a long journey.

At the same time, in his hurry to escape he had thought of nothing except to take his money from the drawer in which his valet had put it.

Because she was frightened at the appearance of the Highwaymen, Carita moved swiftly to his side.

The two Highwaymen swung off their horses and the one nearest to them said in a rough voice:

"Gimme everythin' ye've got on yer, or Oi'll blow yer 'ead off!"

"An' we'll take t'horses," the other man added. "They be a damn' sight better'n ours!"

"Aye – that goes wi'out sayin'!" the first Highwayman affirmed. "So hurry up abaht it, we don' wanna 'ang about 'ere!"

The other man came to stand beside him while their horses started to crop the grass.

"They looks as though they've got a few 'Jimmy-o-Goblins' on 'em!" he said, "an' I wouldn' say no to a kiss from that there gal."

"Get th' money first," the other Highwayman ordered.

He waved his pistol under the Earl's nose and said:

"Come on! Cough oop! Ye know wot us wants!"

The Earl put his hand into his pocket.

Carita was afraid they would take *Mercury* away and she would never see him again.

She wanted to scream and cry, and beg them not to do so.

But because the Earl was standing still without speaking she knew that she too must be brave.

At the same time, when the Highwayman said he

wanted to kiss her she could not help moving nearer to Darol.

The Earl pulled his purse from his pocket.

It was as full as it had been when Carita had hidden it in the drawer in her bedroom.

The only money he had spent had been what he had given to Mrs. Johnson.

At the size of the purse, which was an expensive one, the first Highwayman's eyes brightened.

The other man moved forward to take it.

It was then the Earl opened the purse and poured its contents on the ground.

As the golden sovereigns catching the sunlight slid like a stream onto the grass the two men looked down.

As they did so the Earl with incredible swiftness reached out and seized each Highwayman by the back of the neck.

Violently he smashed their faces against each other.

He did it with his whole strength and both men gave a stifled shriek at the pain.

It was then, as the first Highwayman, half-blinded and with blood already pouring from his nose bent back that the Earl hit him on the point of the chin.

It was with the expertise of an accomplished Pugilist.

He lifted the man into the air and he crashed down onto the ground unconscious.

The other Highwayman was hardly aware of what was happening.

As he opened his eyes he received first a punch to the body from the Earl's left fist.

Then he too had one on the point of the chin which knocked him out.

They both had dropped their pistols.

The Earl picked them up and flung them into a

thick clump of bushes a little below where they were standing.

Without pausing he went to the Highwayman's horses and pulled off their bridles.

He slapped them on the buttocks and the horses reacted by galloping down the incline into the valley.

It all happened so quickly that Carita could hardly believe what she was seeing.

As the horses galloped away she bent to pick up the money.

But he took her by the hand and drew her across the grass towards *Jupiter* and *Mercury*.

At his whistle *Jupiter* came trotting towards them.

As if he knew that he too was wanted *Mercury* came behind him.

Only as the Earl bent to pick Carita up in his arms and lift her onto the saddle did she say:

"Your money . . your money! Darol . . you have . . left it . . behind!"

"Forget it!" he said sharply. "Let us get away from here as quickly as possible!"

Because she was afraid the men might revive and threaten them again Carita was only too willing.

The Earl set off at a gallop and she followed him.

He rode for some distance before he drew *Jupiter* to a halt.

Then as she moved *Mercury* beside him she asked:

"How could . . you have been . . so clever . . so strong and . . so wonderful I was . . desperately afraid . . that they would . . steal *Mercury*!"

The Earl thought any other woman would have been terrified for herself.

He realised however that in her innocence Carita had no idea of what might have happened.

He merely said as they continued to ride:

"Now you understand why you cannot possibly travel alone without protection."

"You . . are right . . of course you are . . right," Carita agreed. "I am so very . . very grateful that . . you were . . there to . . save *Mercury*."

The Earl did not reply.

As they went on Carita felt the shock of what had happened make her feel faint.

She knew however that Darol was determined to ride quickly to where he thought they would be safe, so she said nothing.

She only bent forward to pat *Mercury* on his neck.

She said a little prayer of gratitude that he had not been stolen from her.

The Earl kept up a good pace until just ahead he saw a wood that was on the boundary of his Estate.

They had almost reached the end of their journey.

He then began to wonder if it would be safe for him to go directly to The Priory.

He calculated that Imogen would have gone first to London to seek him out.

She would now have had time to come to the Priory expecting to find him there.

He also wondered if any of his relatives who were always welcome, were visiting him.

It would be asking for trouble if they saw him arrive with anybody as beautiful as Carita and unchaperoned.

He knew exactly what they would surmise and, if the relative was a woman, how she would treat Carita.

Carita would not understand for the simple reason that it did not occur to her to think of him as an attractive man with whom she should not be alone.

He knew she thought of him only as a kind man who

had providentially saved her from the horror of being captured by her Stepfather.

"I must first find out if The Priory is empty," he thought to himself. "Then I shall decide where to take Carita."

They rode through the wood.

Then the Earl, who knew every inch of his Estate, rode towards the Park that was in front of the house itself.

As they emerged from another wood Carita saw the great oak trees under which a number of spotted deer were grazing.

The Earl also saw something moving in the distance.

A few seconds later he saw it was a travelling-carriage passing down the drive.

It had two out-riders on either side of it and was drawn by four horses.

He did not need to have a second glance.

He recognised the livery of the coachman on the box and knew both who owned the carriage and who was inside it.

It was in fact one of his own vehicles which were kept in the Mews behind his house in Berkeley Square.

He was well aware that sitting in it would be Imogen.

She would merely have informed his servants that she wished to visit him at The Priory.

The Earl's mouth was set in a tight line and his eyes were dark with anger.

He guessed that Imogen would not be alone: she would be accompanied by her two disreputable brothers.

If they did not find him as they expected to at The Priory they would simply insist on waiting for him to return.

The servants who had seen Imogen frequently before, would obey her instructions.

For some moment he stared with unseeing eyes ahead of him without speaking.

Then Carita said in a nervous little voice:

"Is . . is . . something . . wrong . . are you . . angry?"

With an effort the Earl replied:

"I was only wondering where I should take you."

"Oh . . please," Carita pleaded, "if I am a nuisance . . I will just ride on. You have been so . . kind . . so wonderfully . . marvellously kind to me . . but I would not . . wish to be a . . burden to you."

The Earl looked closely at her as if to be certain she was sincere in what she was saying.

He found it hard to believe that any woman could be so unselfish.

Or that after such a frightening experience could still be prepared to go on alone.

Then as he looked into Carita's eyes he knew she was not lying to him.

Because she looked so lovely in the sunshine coming through the trees he smiled at her.

"I am going to find somewhere where we can both be safe for another night," he said, "and now I have thought where we can go."

"You are . . sure you want me . . with you?" Carita asked.

"I have no intention of allowing you to face any further danger than we have already encountered."

"I was very . . frightened," Carita admitted, "and think, if they had . . taken *Jupiter* and *Mercury*, how . . unhappy we both would . . have been!"

"I would only have had myself to blame," the Earl said, "for not carrying a pistol with me."

"You were absolutely . . magnificent when you . .

banged those men's heads . . together!" Carita told him. "I could hardly . . believe it was . . happening, but I am very . . sorry that you had to leave . . your money . . behind!"

She paused before she added:

"Of course you have not . . forgotten that I have . . my mother's jewellery with me . . and I owe you . . quite a lot . . already."

"Forget it," the Earl said. "You have to realise that in life we always have to pay for our mistakes."

"Then we must not make any more," Carita said earnestly.

He knew she assumed he was not well off because although he possessed a fine stallion like *Jupiter* he had no groom with him.

His eyes twinkled but he said nothing.

He only rode on to the house where he had decided to take Carita.

Standing on the very edge of the Park it was known as 'Dovecot Cottage' and had been built in the reign of Queen Elizabeth.

The Earl had always thought it one of the most beautiful houses on his estate.

It was quite small.

The Dowager Countess in the reign of Queen Anne had however demanded something far larger and more impressive.

A new Dower House had been built for her.

Dovecot Cottage had been lent over the years to other relatives who were too poor to be able to afford many servants.

They had been pleased to have the small house.

It was a very pleasant place in which to spend the last years of their lives.

When he was trying to think of where to go, the Earl had remembered that his Mother's sister Martha had died six months ago.

She had lived for the last year of her life in Dovecot Cottage.

When his Aunt Martha had asked him where she could go after the death of her husband, he had offered it to her.

Because she was old and frail he had suggested to his Nanny, who was still living at The Priory, that she might look after the old woman.

"You know, Nanny," he said, "I am ready to give you any cottage in the village that takes your fancy, but you refuse to make up your mind."

"What I'm waiting for, Master Darol," Nanny replied, "is to have your son in my arms and see you fill those big Nurseries where you slept as a child. It's a crying shame to see them empty!"

"I am afraid you will have to wait for a long time," the Earl said firmly.

His Nurse had however agreed to look after his Aunt.

She ran the house with the help of two girls from the village.

Then after the old lady's death, she had continued to live there by herself.

The Earl thought now that it was the perfect place for Carita to stay, until he decided how to deal with Imogen.

It was where if necessary, he could hide too.

When they reached the house Carita gave a little cry of excitement.

"It is lovely! Perfectly lovely!" she exclaimed. "It looks as if it has stepped out of a Fairy Story!"

110

The Earl could understand what she was feeling.

The afternoon sun was warm on the red bricks which had turned pink in the passing of the centuries, and glistened on the diamond-paned windows.

As Carita had said, the small but high-chimneyed house did seem unreal and as if it was part of a fairy-tale.

In keeping with its name there had always been white doves in the garden.

They fluttered up onto the roof and down onto the ancient stone sun-dial in the centre of the rose-garden.

The Earl and Carita had reined in their horses and were looking at the house over a well-clipped yew fence.

Then he said:

"If you will wait here, I will go to see if there is anybody inside whom we do not wish to meet. I will not be long."

"I will watch the doves," Carita smiled.

The Earl thought any other woman would have said he must hurry back to her for she would miss him.

As he rode away towards the gate he was aware that Carita actually was watching the doves.

He went up the short drive.

Turning left made his way to the small stable that stood beside the house.

As he expected, there were no horses there and he put *Jupiter* into a stall.

He saw as he did so that there was fresh straw on the floor.

Everything was ready just in case anyone calling should wish to stable their horse while they talked to Nanny.

He walked in through the back-door and along the passage to the small kitchen.

It was where he guessed Nanny would be.

She was sitting at the kitchen-table, a cup of tea in front of her, and was knitting.

She looked up as she heard footsteps on the flagged floor.

When she saw who it was she gave an exclamation of astonishment.

"Master Darol! What are you doing coming to the back-door?"

The Earl walked into the kitchen.

"I want your help, Nanny," he said. "I am in trouble."

"Not again!" Nanny said sharply.

Then as she met his eyes she said:

"Of course I knows that's not what I should be saying to Your Lordship!"

The Earl laughed.

"You can say anything you like, Nanny, as you well know. But I do need your help desperately. Now first, before I say anything else, please call me 'Master Darol' and not 'Your Lordship' and remember that for the moment my name is 'Freeman'."

Nanny stared at him.

"Now what's going on – that's what I'd like to know!" she said.

The Earl sat down at the kitchen-table.

"That is what I'm going to tell you," he said. "And you know, Nanny, you are the only person to whom I can tell the truth."

"So I should hope!" Nanny said quietly. "If I've told you once, I've told you a dozen times – lies come from the Devil himself!"

The Earl laughed. Then he said:

"I am running away, Nanny, because I was nearly tricked into being married to Lady Imogen Basset!"

"That woman!" Nanny snorted. "I'd not have you marrying the likes of her if I had anything to do with it!"

"I agree with you," the Earl said. "I was in a very dangerous situation, but I managed to escape. Then on my way here I had an accident."

"The first thing I noticed when I sees you is that scab on your head! Why can't you take more care of yourself?"

It was just the way Nanny had spoken to him when he was a little boy and the Earl said:

"I was fortunate that it was no worse and I was found and taken to a Farmhouse. While I was there I met a young lady who is also running away!"

Nanny pursed her lips together.

However she did not say anything as the Earl continued:

"Her Stepfather is trying to marry her off to an old man who apparently whips his wives and his horses and she is not unnaturally petrified at the idea of becoming his wife."

"I should think so indeed!" Nanny said.

"When I was unconscious it was she who found me and persuaded two farm boys to carry me in their cart to their farmhouse," the Earl went on. "The Farmer's wife assumed we were a married couple, and because she was afraid of being alone the young lady did not disabuse her."

He thought Nanny was looking somewhat sceptical and he said quickly:

"Carita – that is her name – is very young, very innocent, and at the same time she was very brave a little while ago when we were held up by Highway-men."

"Highwaymen? Whatever next will you be doing, I'd like to know!" Nanny exclaimed.

"I managed to deal with them," the Earl said, "and now I have brought Carita to you where we should both be safe, at least for the moment until I decide how to deal with Lady Imogen. I saw her a few minutes ago arriving at The Priory."

"Without your inviting her?" Nanny asked.

"Definitely without my inviting her," the Earl said, "and while I know why she is there, I am not quite certain yet what I can do about it."

"Well, one thing's for certain, Master Darol, she's not the right person to be your wife – or any other man's for that matter – and that's a fact!"

"Why are you so sure about that?" the Earl enquired out of curiosity.

Then he knew the answer without Nanny telling him the truth.

Servants talk, and Nanny would know everything that he was doing in London.

There were servants who travelled up and down with him.

Also those at the Priory whose relatives – sisters and brothers – were serving among them.

"You are quite right, Nanny," he said. "I made a mistake where she was concerned, and now you have to help me out of it. But no one, and I mean no one, must know I am here, and I want no questions asked about Miss Carita for fear her Stepfather should trace her."

"She'll be safe enough with me," Nanny said with certainty. "As it happens, I told the girls today that as there's so little to do here at the moment they could

114

take two days holiday to see their brother who's just come home from the sea."

"That is certainly helpful," the Earl said, "if you are sure you can manage without them?"

He knew that was a challenge and Nanny tossed her head as she said:

"I'm neither senile nor in me grave. I knows what you likes for your dinner well enough, and that's what you shall have!"

The Earl rose.

"Thank you, Nanny, and do not forget – if Miss Carita asks you, I am 'Master Darol' and on no account refer to me as 'His Lordship' or tell her I am 'The Earl of Kelvindale'."

"I never thought I'd see the day when you'd be ashamed of your own name!" Nanny replied, always determined to have the last word.

The Earl laughed.

"I am putting the horses in the stables. I expect Albert will be coming in to see you, so tell him to look after them, and keep his mouth shut."

Albert was one of the men who worked in the garden.

Also as the Earl knew he had been courting Nanny for over ten years.

He was a man who never said very much at any time.

He was known to be as good with horses as he was with flowers.

There was no better man on the whole Estate.

The Earl left Nanny and walked across the garden.

Carita was still watching the doves.

When she saw the Earl her eyes lit up.

"All is well," the Earl told her.

Carita rode through the gate on *Mercury* and the Earl showed her where to stable him beside *Jupiter*.

As he started to take off the horses' saddles and bridles Carita helped him.

She also put food into the mangers.

The Earl fetched pails of fresh water for them to drink, then shut the doors as she asked:

"Who owns this darling little house?"

"I do," the Earl replied. "And you will find my Nurse inside who looked after me when I was born."

"I suppose I might have guessed that."

"Why?" he enquired curiously.

"Because everything about you is magical. I do not believe you are human."

The Earl laughed as she went on:

"Only a Magician could have coped with two Highwaymen at the same time, and only someone very special – certainly not an ordinary man – could own a house as enchanting as this!"

As the Earl guided Carita through the front-door she said:

"You do not suppose that if I touch anything it will all vanish like Fairy Gold?"

"I sincerely hope not," the Earl replied, "because I am both tired and hungry, as I am sure you are too."

"Just a little," Carita conceded.

As she spoke a door opened and Nanny stood there.

"Come in, Miss," she said to Carita. "Master Darol's been telling me about you, and I promise you'll be quite safe here."

"Thank you," Carita said holding out her hand. "I was just saying that this is a magical place where I am sure no . . one could . . hurt us."

"Not while I'm here!" Nanny said firmly. "I expect you'd like a cup of tea, but first I'll show you to your bedroom. I see you're carrying your saddle-bag."

Carita had taken it from *Mercury*'s back, and now Nanny took it from her.

They walked up the stairs.

There were two quite large bedrooms in Dovecot Cottage and two smaller ones.

The best of them Nanny automatically assigned to the Earl.

The room next to it was very pretty and overlooked the rose-garden.

It had a bow-window, and the sunshine was streaming through the diamond panes making a pattern of gold on the pink carpet.

"I am dreaming!" Carita said. "I know I am dreaming! No room could be as lovely as this!"

"Now you just wash your hands," Nanny said, "and I'll go down and get your tea."

As she went away Carita thought she was hot and dusty and it would take only a moment to slip into one of her muslin gowns.

She hung up her riding-coat with her Mother's brooches in the lining.

She thought with a little shiver that if the Highwaymen had somehow guessed what she was carrying they might have searched her.

She could imagine nothing more horrible than being touched by them.

Then she told herself it was something that had not happened.

Darol had been so wonderful in saving them both so that now they were safe in this enchanted house.

There was therefore no reason for her to go on being afraid.

Then she remembered that her Stepfather would still be looking for her.

"He will . . never . . never find . . me here! Why . . should he?" she asked aloud.

There was a little tremor in her voice.

Almost as if they were replying to her she heard the white doves cooing soothingly to be outside the window.

She was looking at them as she undressed.

She remembered they were special birds that belonged to the gods.

"I am sure they will look after me," she thought, "just as God has looked after me so far, and sent Darol to protect me."

She had a sudden eagerness to be with him and to talk to him.

In fact, to make quite certain he was there and had not, as she feared, disappeared.

When she had put on one of her thin muslin gowns she ran down the stairs to find him.

As she expected, he was in a room which opened out of the hall.

It was a most attractive room with windows on each side of it.

She had eyes only for the Earl however, who was standing looking out into the garden.

Because she was so glad to see him Carita ran towards him.

As she reached him she said in a rapt little voice that seemed somehow to be part of everything around her:

"You are . . here! You are . . really here! Oh . . thank you . . thank . . you for being . . so kind to . . me!"

CHAPTER SIX

Nanny provided an excellent tea despite the fact that she had not been expecting the Earl and Carita.

She quickly made them a few girdle scones, which the Earl had always loved as a boy.

There was hot toast with plenty of butter and honey to spread on it.

There was also the remains of one of Nanny's fruit cakes.

The Earl said it was something he had enjoyed all his life.

Carita thought what fun it was to be having tea with him and that he was in such good spirits.

"I know why you are happy," she told him. "It is because you have come home."

The Earl looked round the small room.

"Would you be happy in such a small place?" he asked.

"I think anyone could be happy here," Carita said, "but what Mama used to say was that it is not bricks and mortar that make a home, but the love which is in it."

The Earl thought that was what he had always wanted for himself.

He did not say so, but rose to his feet.

"I am going to leave you now," he said, "but I know you will be safe with Nanny. I will be back as soon as I can. Do not worry if I am gone for an hour or so."

Carita looked anxious.

"You . . you will . . not be in any danger?" she asked.

"I hope not," the Earl answered, "and when I come back I am sure I will have a lot to tell you."

He looked at her and thought how lovely she was.

Her face was raised to his and her eyes were anxious.

He knew that incredibly it was not anxiety for herself but for him which now made her afraid.

He smiled at her then went into the Kitchen.

"Thank you for a very good tea, Nanny," he said. "I am going now to The Priory, and I may be some time."

Nanny looked at him in surprise.

"I thought you said you were avoiding Lady Imogen!"

"I am not going to see her," the Earl replied, "I only want to know what is going on."

"If you're in hiding, as you say you are," Nanny said, "just be careful. As you well know, there be eyes everywhere watching you."

The Earl laughed.

"I will be careful," he promised.

He went out through the back-door and hesitated for a moment as to whether he should ride *Jupiter*.

Then he told himself that would make him too conspicuous.

Instead he walked into the Park and started to take a round-about route to The Priory.

He went first through the wood and then the shrubbery, avoiding the garden.

120

He finally emerged at the back of the house.

Moving cautiously he found his way to the window he wanted.

He was almost sure that at this time of the day he would find his Secretary, Major Ward, sitting at his desk.

He not only managed The Priory and the Estate, but all his other houses as well.

Major Ward had had a distinguished career as Second in Command in what the Earl's father had always called 'The Family Regiment'.

He had however been injured in the foot when he was serving in Africa and to his great distress had been invalided out of the Army.

He had been delighted to accept the position of Secretary to the Earl of Kelvindale.

Ever since he had come to The Priory he had proved invaluable.

The window was open and looking cautiously into the room the Earl saw the Major at his desk, working on a pile of papers.

To his relief he was alone.

In a low voice he said:

"I am here, Ward!"

The Major started and looked up in astonishment.

He did not for the moment realise that the Earl was outside.

Then as he climbed in through the window he exclaimed:

"I had no idea that Your Lordship had arrived!"

"Lock the door!" the Earl said sharply.

The Major hurried to obey him.

As the key turned in the lock the Earl said:

"Now tell me exactly what is happening. I know Lady

121

Imogen is here. I saw my travelling-chariot bringing her down the drive."

Major Ward looked worried.

"Your Lordship did not expect her to be your guest?"

"I did not invite her," the Earl said briefly, "and I have no wish ever to see her again."

The Major looked even more anxious.

"Her Ladyship said . ." he began.

"That is what I want to know," the Earl interrupted. "Tell me exactly what has happened."

As he spoke he sat down in the only comfortable chair in the room and the Major, standing in front of him, said:

"I was informed about an hour-and-a-half ago that Lady Imogen Basset had arrived from London with both of her brothers."

It was what the Earl had expected, but he said nothing and the Major went on:

"She asked if you were in The Priory, and when she was told you were not, nor were you expected, she said she would wait until you arrived, however delayed you might be."

Again the Earl knew this was to be anticipated.

"She demanded," the Major continued, "the best Guest-Rooms for herself and her brothers and told me, when I went to greet her, that I was to send immediately for the Vicar."

"The Vicar?" the Earl ejaculated.

"I did so without question," the Major said, "assuming it was something Your Lordship had arranged with her."

"And she has seen the Vicar?" the Earl asked.

"Mr. Anderson is with her now," the Major replied, "and . . ."

He paused and the Earl waited until he finished:

". . Her Ladyship has ordered the gardeners to decorate the Chapel."

The Earl was silent and the Major said:

"I can only apologise, My Lord, if this was against your wishes, but Her Ladyship spoke so positively, and I thought, of course, that she was conveying in your absence your own instructions."

Still the Earl did not speak.

Major Ward with a very worried expression in his eyes stood waiting.

He was in fact, devoted to the Earl, as he had been to his father.

He had often worried over his present Master as if he was his own son.

He had watched him grow up and knew what fine qualities there were in young Darol.

Despite his great possessions and his position of importance in the Social World he was still compassionate and understanding to all those who served him.

Major Ward had never known him to do anything mean or ungenerous.

He had often thought that considering the way he had been pursued by women ever since leaving School he had always behaved like a Gentleman.

He was wondering now what on earth could have happened.

Why had the Earl returned to his own house and entered it by climbing through a window?

The Major also questioned what Lady Imogen was up to.

He had never liked her and knew that every servant in the place detested her.

The Earl would have been astounded if he had known

that the Major, who was a regular Churchgoer had been praying every Sunday that he would not marry Lady Imogen.

After what seemed a long silence, the Earl said:

"I wish to speak to the Vicar. Can you manage to get him here without Lady Imogen being aware of what you are doing?"

"Of course I can," Major Ward replied. "I will tell the servants that when he comes out of the small Drawing-Room where he is at the moment with Her Ladyship, I wish to speak to him on a parochial matter."

The Earl nodded.

The Major walked across the room, unlocked the door and went out.

When he had gone the Earl locked it again.

Walking across the room he looked at the maps of the Estate which were hanging on the walls.

He thought as he looked at them how very fortunate he was to own anything which was so very much a part of his family history.

The Priory itself had been in their hands since the Dissolution of the Monasteries.

As the land passed to each succeeding Earl, they had added further acres to it.

It was now undoubtedly the largest Estate in the whole of the County.

He assumed that one day he would hand it on to his son.

But he knew that under no circumstances could his son be born to a woman like Lady Imogen.

Even as he thought of her he could hear Carita's rapt little voice speaking of love.

He knew that for her love was Divine and came from God.

What Imogen felt for him was, he knew, something very different.

He suddenly felt ashamed when he thought of the fiery passions she had evoked in him which were entirely physical.

They had nothing in common with what Carita thought of as love.

He found himself hoping that she would never in the whole of her life encounter women like Imogen.

Nor be aware of the way in which they behaved.

There was a light tap on the door.

He guessed that Major Ward was aware that he had locked it after him.

He unlocked it again and saw the Vicar outside who looked at him in astonishment.

"My Lord!" he exclaimed. "I had no idea you were in the house!"

"Come in, Vicar," the Earl said.

The Vicar obeyed and Major Ward shut the door behind him.

The Earl knew without having to order him to do so that he would be on guard in the corridor outside.

The Vicar, who was an elderly man and the Earl's Private Chaplain, walked further into the room before he said:

"I cannot understand, My Lord! Lady Imogen, to whom I have just been speaking, told me you had not yet arrived. In fact I know she has no idea you are actually in the house!"

"Nobody is aware of it except for Major Ward," the Earl replied. "Now, sit down, Vicar and tell me exactly what Lady Imogen said to you."

The Vicar looked at the Earl with a puzzled expression on his face.

Then as he realised he was waiting, he said:

"Her Ladyship told me you were to be married the moment you arrived home, even if it was late at night."

He saw the expression on the Earl's face and drew in his breath before he went on bravely:

"She said I must hold myself in readiness to come to the Chapel the moment she sent for me. I thought it very strange My Lord, but I understood she was following your precise instructions."

"It is what I expected," the Earl said, "and now, Vicar, I will tell you what I want."

. . . .

When the Earl had left Dovecot Cottage Carita helped Nanny clear away the tea-things.

She would have assisted her with the washing-up but Nanny said:

"Now you go and rest while Master Darol's away. He'll be gone for some time, and if you puts your feet up and shut your eyes you might be able to have a nap."

"You are certain you can manage without me?" Carita asked.

Nanny laughed.

"I've been managing on me own for more years than I care to remember and I've so little to do now that time lies heavy on me hands."

She put the cups and saucers into a large bowl as she went on:

"As I've said to Master Darol time and time again, I've no wish to retire. What I'm waiting for is to look after his son – and the sooner he has one the better!"

There was a pause before Carita remarked:

"He must have been a very attractive little boy."

"That he was!" Nanny agreed. "Everybody spoilt him and who could help it? He had only to smile at them, and they were ready to give him anything he wanted!"

"I am sure you must have loved him very much."

"I wanted him to be happy," Nanny answered firmly. "That's what I want now, but he'll not find happiness with the sort of women as pursue him as if he were a fox!"

Carita suddenly felt her spirits droop.

There was something like a knife turning in her breast.

Of course Darol must have been pursued by women.

How could he help it when he was so handsome, so attractive, and at the same time so kind?

"I think I will go to lie down," she said.

"There's a comfortable sofa in the Sitting-Room," Nanny answered, "or if you prefer, pop into bed."

"I will go to the Sitting-Room," Carita replied. "I want to be there when he returns."

She left the kitchen as she spoke.

Nanny looked after her with an expression in her eyes that would have surprised the Earl.

She was telling herself with a little sigh that he was now a man and must make up his own mind.

Nothing she could say would make any difference.

All the same she found herself wishing that he was small again.

She would give him a shake and tell him that she knew what was good for him!

. . . .

Carita went into the Sitting-Room and thought again how pretty it was.

There was a deep sofa on one side of the fireplace.

Because she was actually rather tired, she put her head on a soft cushion and lifted up her feet.

She was resting comfortably.

Through the open window she could hear the cooing of the doves as they were going to roost.

Only Darol could have owned a place that was so enchanting, she thought.

Then she wondered if he had brought many other women here.

Again the pain was back in her breast.

He would have been as kind to them as he had been to her.

Perhaps when they had been together in this lovely room he had kissed them.

She wondered what it would be like to be kissed.

Then as she wished that Darol would kiss her just once before she had to go away, she knew that she loved him.

She loved him, but she had to leave him and she would never see him again.

'I shall . . never love . . any other . . man,' she thought despairingly before she fell asleep.

. . . .

Walking back the same way he had come, the Earl told himself he had settled everything in a very satisfactory manner.

The Vicar had agreed to everything he had asked for.

When he left the Earl had given a number of instructions to Major Ward.

"I cannot say, My Lord," he said truthfully, "that I am looking forward to what you are asking me to do."

"Nevertheless, I know you will not fail me," the Earl said. "You have always got me out of scrapes in the past!"

He thought as he spoke how cleverly Major Ward had coped with his 'scrapes' when he was a boy.

There had also been one or two early love-affairs which he had had no wish for his father to know about.

The Major had always offered him good advice and he had often been a 'life-line' to a drowning man.

"I will do my best, My Lord," the Major promised now, "but as you must by now be aware, Lady Imogen is a very determined and dangerous woman."

The Earl did not reply.

He merely left the room the way he had entered it, by the window.

As he disappeared into the bushes the Major first sighed, then he gave a short sharp laugh.

He thought that only the Earl could get into trouble so easily, and then manage to extricate himself with the same ease.

. . . .

As he walked back through the wood, the Earl felt the beauty of it sweep away his apprehension.

Also the anger he had felt burning in him ever since he had left *The Towers*.

He was home, his feet were on his own soil.

The last rays of the sun were shimmering through the leaves of his own trees.

"I am so lucky," he told himself, "so incredibly, marvellously lucky! I must never forget to be grateful for it!"

He thought of how Carita had prayed for their safety and some means of escape.

Her prayers had been answered.

Prayer he thought, was as much a part of her whole being as her breathing.

It had no relation to the lip-service that so many women gave to God.

They attended a Service on Sunday because it was fashionable and expected of them.

He told himself he was prepared to believe, as Carita did, that there was a Guardian Angel looking after each of them.

Perhaps, as she also believed, her mother and his mother were guiding and helping their children.

He heard the rooks going to roost in the Park.

Some of the deer were already asleep under the trees.

As he reached Dovecot Cottage he noticed first the doves fluttering agitatedly above the roof.

He wondered what had disturbed them.

He looked over the yew hedges and saw there was a carriage outside the front-door.

He felt himself stiffen.

At the same time, he was aware it was not a carriage he had ever seen before.

Nor did he recognise the servants' livery.

He entered by the garden-gate and walked quickly towards the front-door.

It was open, and as he entered the hall he heard Carita scream.

. . . .

Carita had slept for nearly two hours.

She had no idea that Nanny had peeped into the room and moved quietly out again.

She had then gone into the garden to pick some lettuces for dinner.

She looked to see if there was anything else she could use which Master Darol would enjoy eating.

She had therefore not heard the carriage draw up to the front-door or the rat-tat on the knocker.

It had however awoken Carita.

When she opened her eyes she wondered where she was.

She had been dreaming of Darol, but when she looked round the room he was not there.

She thought he must have been away for a long time and hoped that nothing was wrong.

She sat up on the sofa.

She thought she heard a door opening in the hall and got eagerly to her feet.

He was back and now there would be no need to worry about him.

But when the door of the Sitting-Room opened she gave a little cry of horror.

It was not Darol who stood there, but her Stepfather.

For a moment she could only stare at him.

Then, as a fear like fork-lightning streaked through her body, he gave an exclamation and advanced towards her.

He was looking, she thought, in that small room, very frightening.

More aggressive and even more unpleasant than she remembered.

"So, here you are, Carita," he said in a harsh voice, "and a pretty dance you've led me!"

He came nearer still before he said:

"How dare you run away in that disgraceful fashion! You've caused me a great deal of trouble and expense!"

"H.how have you . . found me, Step-papa?" Carita asked.

She felt as if the world had crashed around her and the ceiling had fallen on her head.

Her whole body was trembling.

"You may well ask that question," Sir Mortimer said. "You may have thought *you* could hide in that sneaky fashion from me, but you could not hide *Mercury*!"

He paused to snarl at her:

"No, my girl, you were not clever enough to hide him. As soon as I learnt what one of my people said he had seen on a certain farm, I took the trouble to go there myself."

Carita gave a little exclamation.

She realised that following Darol's suggestion she had left *Jupiter* and *Mercury* loose in the paddock, and they had been seen there.

How she could have been so stupid as not to be aware that two such outstanding horses would attract the attention of any passer-by.

Especially one who was searching for her.

"I went to the trouble to find you and what did I learn?" Sir Mortimer went on. "Some damned nonsense about your being a married woman and and having a man with you! What man, and where did you find him? That is what I want to know – and make no mistake, I will deal with him as I will deal with you."

Carita gave a little cry.

"It was not his . . fault," she said. "He had an accident . . he was . . unconscious. The Farmer's wife . . assumed that we were . . man and wife . . and that made it . . possible for me to stay the night . . at the farm."

"And you thought you had been clever enough to get away from me and Lord Stilbury!"

"I told you . . Step-papa . . that I would not . . marry him!"

Sir Mortimer laughed, and it was a very ugly sound.

"So you are still attempting to defy me, are you? Well, it will not take me long to beat some sense into you, and don't say I did not warn you!"

He stopped speaking a moment before he said sternly:

"You're coming back with me now, my girl, and after the trouble you've caused me, I promise you will find your punishment a very painful one!"

Carita was trembling.

At the same time, she made one last effort to defy him.

"Whatever you say . . whatever you do . . Step-papa . . I will not marry . . Lord Stilbury!"

"We'll see abut that!" Sir Mortimer said. "And just to give you a taste of what is in store for you, I will give you a sample of it now!"

She saw as he spoke that he carried in his hand a whip with a long thin lash.

It was what he used on his horses and on his dogs.

She tried to evade him, but he caught her by the arm.

Raising the whip above his head he brought it swishing down on her back.

It cut through the thin muslin of her gown and she screamed.

"How d'you like that?" Sir Mortimer roared, "and I intend to give you a dozen of the same every day until you promise to marry the man I've chosen for you!"

He raised his arm again and Carita cringed and twisted to be free.

Before he could strike her for the second time however, the door burst open.

The Earl came into the room.

As he saw what was happening he exclaimed furiously:

"What the Devil do you think you are doing?"

Because he was so impressive and his voice rang out with an authority Sir Mortimer did not expect, he lowered his arm.

As the grip of his other hand relaxed Carita managed to twist herself free.

She rushed to the Earl and flung herself upon him.

"Save me . . oh, save me!" she cried. "My Stepfather had . . found me and he is . . t.taking me away!"

She clung to the Earl who was looking at Sir Mortimer in a manner which made the older man feel slightly uncomfortable.

In an effort to assert himself he said:

"I do not know who you are, but I'm told you have been pretending to be the husband of my Stepdaughter. I could take you in front of the Magistrates for kidnapping a minor!"

"I . . I told . . him," Carita said frantically, "that it was . . not . . your fault . . and you were . . unconscious . . do not let him . . hurt you . . but he says he is taking me . . back to m.marry Lord Stilbury!"

The words were almost incoherent.

Tears were running down her cheeks and the weal on her back was terribly painful.

The Earl looked at her before he said:

"Go upstairs to your bedroom, Carita, I will settle this."

He spoke quietly but in a way which made her know she had to obey him.

Without replying she ran to the door.

134

She opened it and there was the sound of her footsteps running across the hall.

"You needn't waste your time in placating her," Sir Mortimer sneered. "You know as well as I do that the law is on my side, and I'm taking her back with me immediately. If necessary my servants will assist me!"

The Earl knew they consisted of three men.

He would not be able to defend himself against such unequal odds.

He walked across the room to stand in front of the fireplace.

He was aware as he did so that Sir Mortimer was slightly nonplussed by his self-control and composure.

He had obviously expected that 'Freeman' would cringe before him or would at least be obsequious.

"Now look here, young man," he said 'I'm having no nonsense from you! I expect my Stepdaughter has told you that I have arranged a marriage for her. What woman could ask more than to have a rich and titled husband?"

"I am glad you said that," the Earl replied, "because, as it happens, that is exactly what Carita has!"

Sir Mortimer stared at him.

"I do not understand what you are saying!"

"I am telling you that I have married your Step-daughter! She is, I assure you, my wife!"

"I do not believe you!" Sir Mortimer spluttered. "It is impossible for you to have done so!"

"On the contrary, we were married as soon as we left the Farm."

"It is illegal!" Sir Mortimer shouted. "Illegal because as her Guardian I've not given my permission! I swear I will have you thrown into prison where you will not be able to make any more trouble for me or for Carita. She shall suffer for this – yes, by God, she shall suffer for leading me such a dance!"

There was an evil expression on Sir Mortimer's face which made the Earl want to strike him.

Instead, still in the same quiet, authoritative voice he said:

"There is really nothing you can do except I suppose, to take your case to the House of Lords. That will cost you a great deal of time as well as a very large amount of money."

Sir Mortimer had opened his lips to swear at him, but in mid-speech was arrested.

"The House of Lords?" he questioned.

"You have not troubled to ask my name, so perhaps you are unaware that I am in fact the Earl of Kelvindale."

For a moment Sir Mortimer seemed frozen to the floor.

Then he spluttered:

"I – I do not believe it! You are lying – of course you are – lying!"

"I am telling you the truth," the Earl said in a bored voice, "and if you want confirmation of it, it will be quite easy for you to obtain it from anybody in this village, which in fact belongs to me."

"The – the Earl of Kelvindale?" Sir Mortimer croaked. "I suppose that I have seen you on a Race-Course!"

"That is quite possible," the Earl agreed. "I own a number of race-horses, and if you are a racing man you must be aware that I won the Gold Cup at Ascot last month."

Sir Mortimer was astounded.

He stared and stared at the Earl as if he suspected he was being tricked.

At the same time he could not imagine how.

"I – suppose I – recognise you," he said grudgingly, "but why the hell have you married my Stepdaughter?"

The Earl smiled.

"I doubt if you would understand, even if I told you," he said. "And now as we are on our honeymoon, I hope you will be tactful enough to leave us in peace. You have, I understand, frightened my wife in the past, but that is something you will not be able to do in the future!"

"Well, My Lord," Sir Mortimer said in a different tone, "if you have really married my Stepdaughter, then of course, I . ."

"As I have already said," the Earl interrupted, "we are on our honeymoon, and I think even the most thick-skinned interloper would appreciate that we wish to be alone."

The Earl looked Sir Mortimer up and down somewhat contemptuously before he added:

"Good day to you! There is nothing more to be said!"

Stunned and bewildered, still feeling perhaps he was being hood-winked, Sir Mortimer could only walk towards the door.

His shoulders sagged.

He seemed for the moment as if all the stuffing had gone out of him.

As he reached the door he turned back.

The Earl was still standing in front of the fireplace.

He did not speak, but his eyes met Sir Mortimer's and the older man knew he was defeated.

He was thinking vaguely that somehow he must

ingratiate himself with a man he would be even more delighted to speak of as 'to all intents and purposes my son-in-law'.

But even he was aware that this was not the moment.

He was vividly conscious of how he had struck Carita with the whip he held in his hand.

Walking from the room he crossed the hall to let himself out.

Once outside he was helped into his carriage by his footmen.

As he drove away, Sir Mortimer was muttering to himself.

He had beaten Carita.

He was now wondering frantically what he could do that would convince the Earl of Kelvindale that he regretted that action.

He could not find an answer.

CHAPTER SEVEN

The Earl waited until he heard the wheels of Sir Mortimer's carriage being driven away.

Then he glanced out of the window and saw Nanny at the end of the garden.

She had obviously not been aware of anything that had happened.

He went from the Sitting-Room up the stairs and opened the door of Carita's bedroom.

She had been crying and there was an expression of despair on her face.

She looked up as he entered.

Then gave a little murmur that was like that of a child in trouble and ran frantically towards him.

As she reached him she put her hands on his shoulders and looked up at him beseechingly.

He realised she was expecting him to say that she would have to go away with her Stepfather.

Instead he put his arms around her, drew her closer then his lips were on hers.

He felt the start she gave, then her body seemed to melt into his.

Her mouth was very soft, sweet and innocent.

He kissed her at first gently, but there was an ecstasy

rising within her that seemed to pass from her lips to his.

It was different from anything he had ever experienced before.

He drew her closer and still closer and his kiss became more possessive, more demanding.

For Carita it was as if the Gates of Heaven had opened.

She had been quite sure that her Stepfather would take her away.

She had been praying that Darol would kiss her just once before she left, so that she would have something to remember.

'I will . . have to . . kill myself,' she thought. 'I cannot . . think how I . . can do it, but because I love Darol no . . other man shall ever . . touch me!"

Now Darol was kissing her and it was even more wonderful, more perfect than she had imagined it could be.

The pain in her breast had gone.

Instead there was a rapture such as she had never experienced before which carried her into the sky.

Darol raised his head to look down at her, and saw her face had been transformed.

He had never imagined any woman could look so radiant, so unbelievably lovely.

He knew without being told that this was love.

Without speaking he kissed her again, and now she was completely a part of him as no other woman had ever been in the past.

Finally when his lips released her again, she said in a voice that sounded as if it were the song of the angels:

"I . . I prayed . . and prayed . . that you would . .

kiss me . . just once . . before I have to . . leave you."

"Your Stepfather has gone," the Earl said quietly.

"W.without . . me? Must I . . follow him?"

"You need never see him again."

Carita stared at him incredulously.

"You mean . . ? I do . . not understand . . how can you have . . made him go?"

"He left," the Earl said slowly, "because I told him that you and I were married."

"And . . he believed . . you?"

"I made him believe me."

"But he will . . find out it is . . not true. Oh . . help me . . now I have . . time to hide . . tell me where I . . can go!"

"You will be quite safe with me."

She looked at him wide-eyed.

"That . . would be . . absolutely wonderful . . but my Stepfather will come back . . and if I am . . here he will . . find me."

"I told him we were married," the Earl repeated.

"It was very . . kind of you to . . say that . . but I am . . sure he will make . . enquiries to be . . quite certain it is . . true."

"Then we have to make sure he finds it is true, and not a lie," the Earl said.

He felt Carita stiffen.

Then she said in a very frightened little voice:

"W.what . . are you . . s.saying to . . me?"

"I am saying, my darling," the Earl replied, "that I love you and I think you love me a little."

"I love you with . . all my heart . . with every breath I take . . but I . . I never . . thought you would . . love me."

"Nevertheless, I do love you!" the Earl replied. "Do you think that you would be happy with me for the rest of your life?"

"To be . . with you . . even for a short time . . would be like Heaven!" she answered. "I thought . . when I had . . to leave you . . that I must . . d.die!"

The Earl's arms tightened about her.

"You are not going to die, you are going to live, and we have a great many things to do."

"I . . I will look after you," Carita said, "and try to . . make sure that . . no one ever . . hurts you."

The Earl smiled.

"That is what I should be saying to you! However we both have the same idea, I think, my precious, we shall be very happy."

Carita gave a little sob and hid her face against his shoulder.

"It . . cannot be true . . I must be . . dreaming!"

"We will dream together," the Earl said, "but first, my darling, we are to be married very, very soon. I dislike telling lies, and also I want to make sure that if your Stepfather does make enquiries he will find that you really are my wife, and there is nothing he can do about it."

"You are . . sure . . quite sure?" Carita asked.

"As soon as we are married, which will be in a few hours time," the Earl said, "there will be no need for you ever again to be frightened."

He kissed her very gently before he said:

"Now I am going to talk to Nanny while you rest until she comes to help you dress for our wedding."

Carita looked up at him as if she could hardly understand what he was saying.

The Earl bent his head and kissed her again.

Then, as if he could not help himself, his kiss became passionate and demanding.

Carita felt as if the room was swinging dizzily around her.

He picked her up in his arms and laid her down on the bed.

"Rest, my sweet," he said, and his voice was unsteady.

Before she could make any reply he went from the room.

It was then, because Carita was pulsating from his kisses and felt as if the angels were singing, that she put her hands up to her face.

She was saying over and over again:

"Thank You . . God . . Thank You . . Thank You!"

. . . .

The Earl went downstairs to the kitchen where Nanny was preparing dinner.

"Oh, you're back, Master Darol!" she exclaimed.

"I am back, Nanny," the Earl replied.

"Well, I'm wonderin' what's happening."

The Earl looked to where he saw two suit-cases in a corner of the kitchen.

"Major Ward brought those a few minutes ago," Nanny told her, "and says – 'These are for Master Darol'. Why is he calling you Master Darol I'd like to know, talking as if he had known you since you were a baby!"

The Earl laughed.

"I told you I was in hiding, Nanny, and Major Ward is the only person besides yourself who knows where I am."

Nanny looked slightly placated, but she said:

"If them's your evening-clothes as the Major's

brought you, you'll have to dress yourself! I can't prepare the dinner and give you a hand!"

"You may be surprised to hear," the Earl said with a smile, "that I am quite capable of 'dressing' myself, as you call it."

"What's more, the Major says to me, he said," Nanny went on, "I was to open the small case while you were at dinner and I'd know what to do with it. What did he mean by that?"

"Exactly what he said," the Earl answered, "and he was following my instructions."

"I don't know what's going on, that I don't!" Nanny expostulated. "I'm not sure if I'm on my head or my heels!"

"I promise you everything will be made clear to you when you open the case that has been left for you," the Earl said.

He smiled when he saw the curiosity in Nanny's eyes and picking up the larger case he went upstairs to his bedroom.

A little later Nanny took some hot water up to Carita.

She was lying on her bed looking so radiantly happy that for the moment it took Nanny's breath away.

"If you're going to change for dinner, Miss Carita," she said, "you'd better hurry if you won't want what I've cooked for you to get cold."

"No, of course not," Carita replied.

She got off the bed and started to undress while Nanny took a white gown out of the wardrobe.

She had pressed it.

Although it was very plain and simple she thought as Carita was looking so lovely at the moment it did not matter what she wore.

144

She had brought with her the smaller of the two suit-cases that had been left in the kitchen.

When she put it down Carita asked:

"What have you got there, Nanny?"

"I've no idea!" Nanny replied tartly. "The Master's ordered that I'm not to open it until you're at dinner."

Carita was hardly listening as Nanny buttoned up her gown.

She could only say:

"I am so happy . . so wonderfully . . wonderfully happy!"

The way she spoke was obviously very different from the way Nanny had heard her speak before.

She looked at her reflection in the mirror before she asked:

"Are you tellin' me that Master Darol has said something special to you?"

"He loves me! Oh, Nanny, he loves me, and I am the happiest woman in the whole world!"

"There now!" Nanny exclaimed. "If that isn't the most sensible thing I've heard in a long time! It's what he's always wanted – someone like yourself to look after him and keep those nasty women away."

"That is what I will try to do . . you know I . . will."

As Carita finished speaking she kissed Nanny on the cheek.

Then she ran from the room as if she could not wait any longer to be with the man she loved.

He was waiting for her in the Sitting-Room.

As she came in through the door and saw him for the first time in his evening-clothes she gave a little gasp because he looked so magnificent.

She also noticed, and it surprised her, that there

were several decorations on the breast of his evening-coat.

Yet because he held out his arms she sped across the room as if she had wings on her feet to reach him.

He kissed her and there was no need for words.

Only when Nanny opened the door to say that dinner was ready did she move away to look at him adoringly.

"I love . . you!" she whispered.

"As I love you!" the Earl replied.

They went into the Dining-Room hand in hand.

Nanny had left everything ready for them.

The mushroom soup was in a china tureen from which they could help themselves.

The next course was chicken done in a special way which the Earl had always enjoyed.

It was in a silver entrée dish over a candle to keep it hot.

But because she felt so happy, Carita hardly knew what she ate.

All she could think of was that she was going to marry the most handsome, attractive and kindest man she had ever met in her whole life.

Only as dinner was finished did she say almost as if she was afraid to ask the question:

"Are we . . really going to be . . married tonight?"

"The carriage will be arriving in a few minutes," the Earl replied, "so go upstairs and see what Nanny has ready for you in your bedroom."

Carita hesitated for a moment.

"You are . . quite . . quite sure . . that it will not hurt you . . in any way to . . marry me? Suppose . ."

"No one will hurt me, or you!" the Earl said firmly. "And if you are asking questions, perhaps I should ask you if you are quite content to marry me rather than the rich and titled man your Stepfather had chosen for you."

"I would marry . . you if you were a . . crossing-sweeper . . or a coal-miner!" Carita said passionately. "And if you can live in this darling little house then I will . . never ask for . . anything else because with . . you I will be . . in Heaven!"

The Earl smiled.

It was what he had always wanted, but what he felt he would never have.

"Then hurry," he said, "for the carriage will soon be here and I would not want to keep the horses waiting."

"No . . of course not," Carita agreed.

She ran up the stairs and burst into her bedroom to find Nanny ready for her.

Draped on the bed was the most magnificent Brussels lace veil she had ever seen.

Nanny was holding in her hands a wreath for her to wear on top of it.

The flowers which would encircle her head were made of diamonds.

"Now I shall really look like a Bride!" Carita cried. "How could Darol have thought of anything . . so wonderful?"

Nanny arranged the veil not over her face, but falling each side so that it almost touched the floor.

The diamonds in the wreath glittered in the candle-light.

It was then Carita remembered her mother's jewellery.

She thought that on her wedding-day she must wear something that had belonged to her mother.

It took her only a few minutes to remove the bracelet from the hem of her riding-skirt.

Nanny took a diamond brooch from the lining of her riding-coat.

"Fancy you putting them there!" she exclaimed.

"They might otherwise have been stolen by Highway-men," Carita said, "but as it was, Darol saved us both. He was magnificent! I wish you could have seen . . the way he . . knocked them both . . unconscious!"

"You'll have to tell me all about it another time," Nanny said.

"Yes, I must not keep him waiting," Carita replied.

"I'll be praying for you both," Nanny promised.

Quite unexpectedly there were tears in her eyes.

"God bless you," she said to Carita, "and you look after my boy."

"You know . . I will."

Carita kissed Nanny and ran down the stairs.

Outside there was a small closed carriage and driving it was Major Ward.

The Earl was thinking how well he had carried out his orders.

He knew, although it would be extremely unpleasant, that the Major would not fail him the next morning.

He had told him that when Lady Imogen called she was to be informed that in an hour a carriage would be waiting.

It would take her and her two brothers back to London.

The reason she was to leave immediately was that the Earl would be arriving later in the day with his wife.

She would understand that as they had only recently been married they would not wish there to be any visitors at the house.

"Supposing she refuses to go?" the Major had asked the Earl.

"In that case you can tell her that the Vicar will verify that the marriage has taken place. If she still refuses to leave, the servants will, on your instructions, place her luggage in the carriage and, if necessary, put her two brothers inside by force!"

The Major had sighed, knowing how unpleasant Lady Imogen could be.

At the same time, he knew the Earl was right.

In those circumstances it would really be impossible for her to stay on.

The Earl was sure it would also be difficult for her to create a scandal about it.

To be thrown out of his house for no good reason might evoke a certain amount of sympathy in the raffish set in which she moved.

But that he was returning home with his Bride would, if Imogen made a scene, make her a laughing stock.

There were a number of people who would be delighted to see her humiliated.

She would be well aware of this.

The Earl was prepared to give her a generous sum of money once she had returned to London.

He knew that that, if nothing else, would ensure her silence.

She would soon find herself another rich man, if not such a distinguished one.

The Earl helped Carita into the carriage and took her hand as they drove off.

He knew how excited she was and he raised her fingers one by one.

"This is an adventure that we shall always remember," he said gently.

"How could . . we . . ever forget . . it?" Carita asked.

They drove in silence until the coach came to a standstill at the back of what Carita realised was a very large house.

She had been aware as they were driving that there were no candle-lanterns on the carriage.

The driver was dependent upon the moon to light his way.

The Earl helped her out, and she saw that in front of them was an arched Gothic door.

The Earl, still holding her hand, led her through it.

There was another door and when it was opened they were in a very beautiful Chapel.

It was lit by dozens of candles and massed with flowers.

Standing in front of the altar was a Parson wearing a white surplice.

The Earl drew Carita slowly up the aisle.

She knew that this was the most wonderful moment of her life.

He was thinking that this was exactly how he wished to be married to somebody he loved and who loved him for himself.

No fashionable friends to criticise or, in his case, feel envious.

'We are alone except for God and our Guardian Angels,' he told himself.

It occurred to him that that was a very strange thing for him to think.

As he had arranged, an ancient groom whom he knew could be trusted was outside holding the horses.

Major Ward was standing in the doorway of the Chapel.

He was the only witness to their marriage.

He would also protect them in case there should be any interference from those staying at The Priory.

The Chaplain read the beautiful words of the Marriage Service with a sincerity that was very moving.

When he joined Darol Alexander and Carita as man and wife they were both sure that the angels were singing.

After the Parson blessed them they were still for a moment. Then the Earl drew Carita to her feet.

Leaving the Chapel with Major Ward they drove back to Dovecot Cottage.

There was a light in the hall, but there was no sign of Nanny.

Carita guessed that she had tactfully gone to bed so that they could be alone.

They went up the stairs together, but when Carita would have gone to her own room the Earl drew her into his.

She had not really seen it before.

She realised now that it was larger than the one where she had slept.

The bed was a four-poster with angels and doves carved on the canopy.

It had belonged to the Earl's grandmother.

As there had been nowhere to put it when she had moved into the Dower House, she had sent it to Dovecot Cottage.

It was the most beautiful bed that Carita had ever seen, but when she was about to say so she suddenly felt shy.

The Earl shut the door.

Now he pulled off his tail-coat with its decorations and flung it down on a chair.

Then he stood for a moment just looking at Carita.

"My wife!" he said very softly.

"Is it . . really . . true?" Carita asked. "Oh . . darling Darol, I am . . so afraid that I am . . dreaming!"

"That is what I am feeling too," the Earl said. "I have looked for you and waited for you, but thought I should never find you."

Before she could answer him he was kissing her.

Then it was impossible either to think, or to speak, but only to know the ecstasy and wonder of love.

. . . .

A long time later Carita whispered against the Earl's shoulder:

"I love you . . and now I know what . . it is to be so . . happy that there are . . no words to . . express it."

"I feel the same," the Earl answered. "I find it hard to realise how blessed I have been in finding you."

Carita gave a little laugh.

"I found you," she contradicted, "when you were unconscious!"

"When I first opened my eyes and saw you looking at me," the Earl said, "I thought you were an angel and I had reached Heaven!"

"How could I have known . . how could I ever have guessed that you would be my . . husband?" she asked.

Then she gave a little cry.

"Do you realise," she asked, "that we have been married, but unless my Stepfather told you, you do not know my full name, and I do not know yours!"

The Earl smiled.

"I wondered when you would ask that."

"Everything . . has happened . . so quickly," Carita

said, "and Nanny just talks of you as 'Master Darol'. So I suppose I . . forgot you must have . . another name."

"Why not tell me yours first?" the Earl suggested, "Incidentally, tomorrow we must add our full names to the Marriage Register in case your Stepfather, or any nosey people, wish to see it."

"Your Parson did not insist on our doing so tonight," Carita remarked.

"I assured him we would do so tomorrow," the Earl explained, "and as he is my Private Chaplain he agreed."

Carita's eyes opened wide with surprise as she repeated:

"Your Private Chaplain?"

"Yes," the Earl replied. "We were married in my own Chapel which is part of The Priory, which is where I live."

There was silence while Carita absorbed this.

Then she asked hesitatingly:

"Then . . you do . . not live . . here?"

"Dovecot Cottage belongs to me, but it is used by my relatives. I hope, however, my darling, you will love my real home as much as I do."

He felt Carita move a little closer to him as if she was afraid.

Then she said:

"I . . I thought you were . . poor . . that we would . . live here . . and I would . . look after you."

"You will have to look after me wherever we are," the Earl said. "I am in fact the Earl of Kelvindale, and Kelvin Priory is one of the oldest and most beautiful houses in the County."

Again there was silence.

Then Carita said:

"P.perhaps you . . should not have . . married me . . but instead somebody . . important."

"I married somebody whom I love with all my heart," the Earl said, "and what is more important than anything else, I believe that she loves me!"

"Oh, I do love you . . I do!" Carita said. "But, darling suppose . . as you are so . . important that I . . fail you and you will . . then regret that you did not marry . . somebody else?"

The Earl laughed and it was a very tender sound.

"Now you are being ridiculously modest," he said. "I have never, Carita, and this is the truth, seen anybody more lovely than you, and no one has ever made me feel so happy or what I felt when I made you mine for all eternity."

"Is that . . really . . true?"

"I swear to you on everything I hold sacred that it is the truth," the Earl answered, "and, darling, you did say it was not bricks and mortar that makes a home – but love!"

"We will . . fill that . . big house with so . . much love that . . nothing else will be of . . any importance," Carita whispered.

The Earl knew it was a vow.

It was what he had wanted to hear and what he had longed for.

It was something he would never lose.

He was only afraid that his relatives, who could be difficult at times, would think that Carita was not socially important enough for him.

He thought her Stepfather was an appalling man.

He hoped none of his Aunts and Cousins would ever come in contact with him.

But he loved Carita with every breath he drew.

As far as he was concerned, whoever her parents were was completely immaterial.

Yet there was a world outside which they would have to face one day.

While he held traditional appointments at Court, so, as the Countess of Kelvindale, would Carita.

"Now that you know who I am," he said gently, "tell me your real identity which you have kept so secret up until now."

"Only because I was . . hiding from . . Step-papa," Carita answered. "My father was Captain Richard Wensley."

"I seem to know the name," the Earl said. "Surely it is strange that you have so few relations, except of course the Uncle you were trying to reach in Norfolk."

"I was afraid . . he would not . . want me," Carita answered, "but he became the . . head of the family . . when he came into the title."

The Earl was still.

"The – title?" he questioned.

"Yes. Uncle Andrew is Lord Wensley of Wen, and the title dates back to the 17th century."

The Earl closed his eyes.

He knew now it would be impossible for his family to criticise or in any way hurt Carita.

He could only think that once again his luck had not failed him.

He was in fact the most fortunate man whom Fate had ever smiled upon.

He drew Carita closer to him and said:

"Now that we are formally introduced, may I tell you, my beautiful, perfect little wife, that I adore and worship you, and all I want to do is to make love to you from now until the end of our lives."

Carita put her arms around his neck.

"That is . . what I wanted to . . say to . . you," she whispered, "and . . darling . . as your . . house is . . very big, we must have . . lots of . . children to . . fill it."

She hid her face against him before she went on:

"First of course . . we must have a son . . for Nanny to look after . . and who will be . . exactly like you . . handsome, clever and very . . very . . kind . ."

It was impossible to say any more for the Earl was kissing her; kissing her eyes, her cheeks, her lips, her neck and her breasts.

Then the stars seemed to envelop them and they were swept up into a special Heaven of their own.

There they would know no fear, only the real true love which comes from God.

It is what all men and women seek and which those who are pure in heart find.

Cartoons:

Barbara Cartland Romances (Book of Cartoons)
has recently been published in the U.S.A., Great Britain,
and other parts of the world.

Children:

A Children's Pop-Up Book: "Princess to the Rescue"

Cookery:

Barbara Cartland's Health Food Cookery Book
Food for Love
Magic of Honey Cookbook
Recipes for Lovers
The Romance of Food

Editor of:

"The Common Problem" by Ronald Cartland (with a preface by the
Rt. Hon. the Earl of Selborne, P.C.)
Barbara Cartland's Library of Love
Library of Ancient Wisdom
"Written with Love" Passionate love letters selected by Barbara
Cartland

Drama:

Blood Money
French Dressing

Philosophy:

Touch the Stars

Radio Operetta:

The Rose and the Violet
(Music by Mark Lubbock) Performed in 1942.

Radio Plays:

The Caged Bird: An episode in the life of Elizabeth Empress of
Austria.
Performed in 1957.

Sociology:

You in the Home

The Fascinating Forties

Marriage for Moderns

Be Vivid, Be Vital

Love, Life and Sex

Vitamins for Vitality

Husbands and Wives

Men are Wonderful

Etiquette

The Many Facets of Love

Sex and the Teenager

The Book of Charm

Living Together

The Youth Secret

The Magic of Honey

The Book of Beauty and Health

Keep Young and Beautiful by Barbara Cartland and Elinor Glyn

Etiquette for Love and Romance

Barbara Cartland's Book of Health

General:

Barbara Cartland's Book of Useless Information with a
   Foreword by the Earl Mountbatten of Burma.
   (In aid of the United World Colleges)

Love and Lovers (Picture Book)

The Light of Love (Prayer Book)

Barbara Cartland's Scrapbook
   (In aid of the Royal Photographic Museum)

Romantic Royal Marriages

Barbara Cartland's Book of Celebrities

Getting Older, Growing Younger

Verse:

Lines on Life and Love

Music:

An Album of Love Songs
sung with the Royal Philharmonic Orchestra

Films:

A Hazards of Hearts

The Lady and the Highwayman

A Ghost in Monte Carlo

A Duel of Love

Other books by Barbara Cartland

Romantic Novels, over 400, the most recently published being:

A Game of Love
The Sleeping Princess
A Wish Comes True
Loved for Himself
Two Hearts in Hungary
A Theatre of Love
A Dynasty of Love
Magic from the Heart
The Windmill of Love

Love Strikes Satan
The Earl Rings a Belle
The Queen Saves the King
No Disguise for Love
Love Lifts the Curse
Too Precious to Lose
A Tangled Web
Just Fate
A Miracle in Mexico

The Dream and the Glory
(In aid of the St. John Ambulance Brigade)

Autobiographical and Biographical:

The Isthmus Years 1919–1939
The Years of Opportunity 1939–1945
I Search for Rainbows 1945–1976
We Danced All Night 1919–1929
Ronald Cartland (With a foreword by Sir Winston Churchill)
Polly – My Wonderful Mother
I Seek the Miraculous

Historical:

Bewitching Women
The Outrageous Queen (The Story of Queen Christina of Sweden)
The Scandalous Life of King Carol
The Private Life of Charles II
The Private Life of Elizabeth, Empress of Austria
Josephine, Empress of France
Diane de Poitiers
Metternich – The Passionate Diplomat
A Year of Royal Days
Royal Lovers
Royal Jewels
Royal Eccentrics